Walter Copland Perry

The Revolt of the Horses

Walter Copland Perry

The Revolt of the Horses

ISBN/EAN: 9783744648219

Printed in Europe, USA, Canada, Australia, Japan

Cover: Foto ©Andreas Hilbeck / pixelio.de

More available books at **www.hansebooks.com**

THE REVOLT OF
THE HORSES

BY

WALTER COPLAND PERRY

LONDON
GRANT RICHARDS
9 HENRIETTA STREET, COVENT GARDEN, W.C.
1898

THE REVOLT OF THE HORSES

CHAPTER I

ABOUT 10° south of the Cape of Good Hope, in 45 deg. S. lat., lies an island which is conjectured to be about 150 miles long and 70 miles broad. The approach to it from the north is rendered extremely difficult by a number of parallel reefs of coral formation, which lurk treacherously at no great depth beneath the surface of the water. There are, however, a few narrow and tortuous channels, just deep enough to float a large boat of moderate draught. The beach, which is covered at high tide, consists of a broad belt of shining sand, or, rather, minute shells, of a rosy hue, beyond which basaltic rocks, varying from 40 ft. to 100 ft. in height rise sheer above the sea. The interior of the country presents the appearance of a vast park of gentle undulating surface, interspersed with groups of lofty forest trees, copses of flowering and fragrant shrubs, and rich parterres of flowers of every form and hue. Here and there the eye met groves of myrtle and orange trees on which

> " . . . fruits and blossoms blushed
> In social sweetness on the selfsame bough."

Sometimes the gentle hills are crowned with

Revolt of the Horses

turret-like rocks, from which flow crystal streams in gay cascade, bringing life and motion into the landscape. The air is bright and luminous, beyond all that the ancient poets sing of the pellucid atmosphere of Athens, and forms a medium by which the sunlight paints the rocks and the unruffled surface of the sea with a never-ending variety of hues— fringing the waves as they kiss the shore with a perpetual rainbow. Gentle rains fall at intervals, but instead of causing annoyance or distress, they only bring refreshment and new sensations of delight. The heavenly bodies move large and bright in the tender azure of the sky, appearing to hang nearer than in other climes, and to look down with love on the fair, dædal land beneath them. The heat of the midday sun, and its brilliant light, which in that transparent atmosphere might be blinding to the eyes, are mitigated and rendered purely pleasurable by soft fleecy clouds; while its rising and setting afford an ever-varying spectacle of ineffable glory and magnificence. And when the flood of liquid gold in which the sun-god has bathed the earth is withdrawn, the moon and stars draw near with their silvery light, and by their milder, but hardly less beautiful, effulgence chase away regret for the departed day. The glowworms then bespangle the emerald grass, the fireflies flit among the leaves, light up the scented shades of the groves, and settle on those delicate and lovely flowers, those darling "children of Mylitta," which shun the day and only expand their scarlet or snow-white pâtisses beneath the gentler light of

2

Revolt of the Horses

the moon.[1] The nightingale and other nocturnal songstresses to us unknown succeed the lark and fill the fragrant air with melody.

The chief inhabitants of this fragment of Paradise, into which no Satan has found an entrance through the heart of woman, are the fitting complements of the lustrous atmosphere, the brilliant colours, and the melodious voices of this favoured region. But they are not *men* : in outward form, at least, they are what we call horses, as was discovered by the first human being who landed on the island, the celebrated traveller, Lemuel Gulliver. He calls them Houyhnhnms, as they call themselves. It would be quite impossible to give an adequate conception of the external form of the Houyhnhnm. We may indeed try to rise to it by contemplating the finest specimens of the English racehorse, or by imagining what an ideal horse from the hand of Pheidias would have been. In this effort of imagination we may derive some aid from the wondrous head of Selene's horse from the pediment of the Parthenon, now in the British Museum. But the grandeur and beauty of his form are the poorest attributes which the Houyhnhnm has received from the lavish hand of nature ; and it requires a still higher flight of fancy to apprehend, even dimly, his intellectual and moral perfections. To the high spirit, the sweet temper, the gentle goodness, the all-enduring patience under suffering, which we see in our own horses, we must add a

[1] These flowers are the Bois chataigne (Carolinea) red, and the Ipomoea (Bona nox) snow-white.

3

Revolt of the Horses

degree of intelligence and virtue to which no human being ever rose.

The very highest intellectual and moral attributes belong, however, to only one class of Houyhnhnms. We do not find among them the infinite variety of breed and size which prevails among our horses, the result of indiscriminate crossing, of different climates, and, above all, of the different treatment they receive at our hands. They only know three sharply distinguished types, which, for want of better terms, though they are somewhat misleading we may call the royal, the aristrocratic, and the working classes. These are outwardly distinguished from one another by colour; the first two being bay, chestnut, or black, and the third white, sorrel, and iron-grey; the two higher classes are poorly represented by our thoroughbreds, and the last by our heavier hunters, carriage, and farm horses. The former alone have those sublimer faculties of mind and soul, which transcend the loftiest human intellect, and the purest and noblest human virtue. The working Houyhnhnms possess what we call good sound sense, perfect sweetness of temper, and kindness of disposition. They find absolute contentment and delight in the interchange of mutual good offices with their equals, and in trustful loving obedience to the higher wisdom of the superior castes.

It is impossible, as we have said, for the human intellect in its purblind gropings, and with its narrow range, to rise to a full conception of the Houyhnhnm nature. We can but faintly trace it by

4

Revolt of the Horses

following the outlines of the noblest forms of humanity in its rarest and happiest development; by raising our eyes to the empyrean sunlit heights at which the most god-like genius, escaping for a few short hours from its shroud of clay, has tremblingly sustained itself. The "fine phrensy" of the poet, the ecstatic rapture of the Christian saint, the visions of ideal beauty, which the inspired artist vainly strives to transfer to marble or to canvas, the thrilling transports of the musical composer, the stately march of the philosophic mind through untrodden fields of thought and knowledge, all these, a thousandfold intensified, belong to the normal state, the daily life of the blessed and gifted Houyhnhnm.

The happiness of the inferior class, though of a less exalted nature, is no less rounded and complete. They enjoy to the full and unalloyed all the pleasures of which they are capable, without either longing or regret. Their days pass tranquilly away in the enjoyment of perfect health, in the free exercise of their limbs, and in light and pleasant occupation in the fields under the direction of their beloved masters.

If anything could disturb the perfect serenity and bliss of this happy community it would be the presence in the island of an inferior race, called Yahoos. These are hideous, malicious, stupid, but cunning creatures in the shape of men, possessed of no redeeming quality, abhorrent alike to the sight, the smell, and the moral sense of the Houyhnhnms. They differ from the latter in

5

almost every conceivable respect. Their existence lies altogether apart from and out of harmony with, the rest of creation. They derive no pleasure from the beauties of nature, or from the exercise of intellectual or moral powers. They are broken up into families, the members of which may unite to injure or destroy those of another family, but are always quarrelling among themselves. When they hold together, it is only for purposes of self-defence, or aggression on the liberty and property of some other household. Sometimes larger combinations of families take place for a time for the purpose of destroying other clans or tribes, or depriving them of some supposed advantage. One nation, if we may call it so, will invade the territory of another, and after butchering the inhabitants, divide the conquered land among themselves. Should they, however, fail in their enterprise, they will return to their own borders and commence a civil war. In fact, were it not for the intervention of the Houyhnhnms and the rapid and reckless propagation of these vile creatures, they would long ago have perished altogether through personal feuds and internecine wars. All their actions may be traced to either greed, lust, or fear. Their life is one long struggle, not only for existence, but for the means of indulging their base appetites. The stronger and more cunning among them amass food in quantities far beyond their wants, which they jealously guard and will allow to perish rather than give away. The males enter into fierce contention with one another for the favour of the female Yahoos, for which, under the sting of a kind of madness which takes complete possession of them, they will kill one another, and even take their own lives. The females delight in being the object of this transient phrensy, and perform the most extraordinary antics to draw the attention of the males. The rivalry among them is so great that if one female Yahoo is suspected of being more attractive than her rivals, they will combine to hunt her down and tear her to pieces with their teeth and claws.

There is some doubt as to the origin of these wretched and noisome animals; some maintaining that they had been generated by the heat of the sun from the corrupted slime of a marsh, or from the ooze and froth of the sea. The most credible tradition is that a pair of these brutes suddenly appeared on a mountain in the interior and multiplied so fast in that genial and productive climate and land, that the Houyhnhnms were obliged to destroy a vast number of them. Some thousands, however, were preserved and employed in raising crops of oats, and generally as beasts of burden, for which their great strength well fits them. Their numbers are strictly limited, and they keep themselves as far as possible out of sight of their masters, that the latter may not be offended by their presence.

The Houyhnhnm nation is governed, or rather advised, by a Committee of Twelve, selected by what we must call the King, for want of some more appropriate word—*i.e.* the chief representative

Revolt of the Horses

of a family in which the highest qualities of the highest class manifest themselves in the greatest perfection. The members of this family are known at once by their form and bearing, and also by the bright white star in the middle of their foreheads. They are supposed to be descended from the horses of the Sun. In one sense, the monarch rules with absolute power; but to our ears the words rule and power convey a false impression. The lofty intelligence of this great chief enables him to know what is best for the community, and his perfect benevolence induces him to carry out his plans with the sole view of conferring happiness. The Committee of Twelve, belonging to the upper class, consult with him for the general good, or rather listen to the decisions at which he arrives—for it is impossible for reasonable beings to differ from them; they are recognised at once as the dictates of the greatest wisdom combined with the most perfect benevolence. These decisions are communicated to the whole nation, and are at once received with admiring acquiescence.

On occasions when matters of great importance are to be brought forward, a general meeting is summoned, not so much for discussion, for there is no difference of opinion, but to give the whole community the pleasure and advantage of hearing the King's views and sentiments from his own mouth.

Such an occasion occurred in the year 1950. The meeting was held in a long, low, oblong

Revolt of the Horses

room of great extent, along the walls of which ran a continuous manger filled with corn, above which was a rack well furnished with fragrant hay. In every part of this vast stable, if we may call it so, Houyhnhnms were to be seen standing singly, or in groups, or lying on litters of fresh, clean straw. In the centre of one of the long sides, on a raised mound of earth, stood the dark bay Houyhnhnm king, Lampros by name, distinguished above the rest by the grandeur of his proportions, and the royal dignity of his bearing. Near him reclined his consort, Leucippe, a mare of the same hue, differing from the King chiefly in the greater slimness and elegance of her form, and the silken texture of her flowing mane. With them were a colt about two years and a half old, called Aethon, and a filly a year younger, both of whom were distinguished by the white star on their foreheads. In front of the raised dais, but not on it, stood a horse and a man, towards whom all eyes were directed and all thoughts turned. The man, who was in the dress of an English traveller, looked shabby and careworn, and was pale with excitement and exhaustion. The horse, though a very fine specimen of an English thoroughbred, contrasted very unfavourably in all respects with the magnificent forms of the Houyhnhnms about him. His sunken head, dim eyes, and drooping tail expressed fear, dejection, and bewilderment; and he gazed with unspeakable astonishment on the Houyhnhnms, in whom he could not but recognise a kindred

9

race.   Near the unfortunate pair were two strongly-built working Houyhnhnms, who, on receiving a sign from the King, proceeded to give an account of a singular occurrence.

It appeared that while the two labouring Houyhnhnms were bathing in the sea in the early morning, they saw a ship at about a mile distant from the shore, which seemed to have stuck fast on a rock and to be exposed to the violence of the waves.   As a ship was to them an unknown object, they stood gazing at it and conjecturing what it might be, when their attention was attracted by two bodies, which were washed up one after another at their feet.   In one of these they recognised an animal of their own species, though in a degraded and miserable form, and in the other a creature resembling a Yahoo in face, but covered with a kind of loose skin, the nature of which they were at a loss to understand.   After lying for some time motionless on the sands as if dead, they were observed to move, and were heard to utter low, moaning sounds as if in pain. The two Houyhnhnms had then summoned a few Yahoos, whom they ordered to take up the horse and man with all care, and bear them to the nearest habitation.   As soon as they were sufficiently recovered corn and water were given to them, which the horse devoured greedily, and on which the Yahoo with some difficulty contrived to feed. The news of this occurrence was brought to the King, who gave orders that they should be brought before him with as little delay as possible.

Revolt of the Horses

Such were the circumstances which preceded the meeting referred to above. When all were assembled the King, in a few short words, explained his reasons for summoning the assembly, and called attention to the singular visitors of their island. He pointed out the extraordinary similarity in the form of the horse to members of their own race. This, he said, was the more remarkable, because he was not only in the company of a kind of Yahoo, but, to all appearance, actually in subjection to this unclean and inferior creature. He anticipated some difficulty in solving the mystery, because it was hardly likely that the horse would possess any knowledge of their language ; and the Yahoo would not have sense enough to give them any information, even if he spoke the same tongue as their own vile slaves. One of the Council of Twelve, who stood near the dais, suggested that the man should be taken out into the fields by a Houyhnhnm, and confronted with a Yahoo, to see whether they could understand one another. This was done, but without effect, for on the man addressing the Yahoo in English, the latter replied by an utterly unintelligible gabble. On the return of the man to the place of meeting, the King addressed a few words to the horse, to which the latter listened with pricked up ears, and then with extreme difficulty, neighed forth a few broken sentences, which all who heard them seemed to understand. A murmur of surprise ran through the whole assembly, which was raised to the

Revolt of the Horses

highest pitch when the man addressed the King in the same debased Houyhnhnm dialect, and begged permission to explain their presence in the island, and the still more extraordinary phenomenon of a Yahoo possessing a knowledge of the language of the country. The request was immediately granted. The Houyhnhnms crowded round the dais with every mark of intense curiosity, and the man in broken sentences, and with frequent pauses, told the following tale:—

"I am," he said, "the great-grandson on the father's side of an Englishman named Gulliver, who, early in the eighteenth century, was set on shore in this island by the mutinous crew of his ship. He had the good fortune to gain the favour of a distinguished Houyhnhnm, who took him into his service. His generous master instead of employing him as a beast of burden, treated him with the greatest consideration, and encouraged him to learn the Houyhnhnm language. During his residence in this blissful land, my ancestor was so deeply impressed by the superiority of your godlike race, that, as far as his nature would allow, he became a Houyhnhnm. He would most gladly have remained here for the rest of his life, but it was deemed inadvisable to allow one, who was, after all, a Yahoo, to live on intimate terms with a Houyhnhnm. It was feared that in spite of his apparent reformation, his innate vicious propensities might one day break forth again, and be a source of evil

12

Revolt of the Horses

and corruption. He therefore left the island with infinite reluctance, and after many adventures reached his native land. But he found it impossible, after his long sojourn in the pure moral atmosphere of Houyhnhnm society, to sympathise again with the low aims, or to bear with the meannesses and vices, of his former associates ; and he dragged out the remnant of his life in a secluded nook of an almost uninhabited island on the west coast of Scotland. There he passed most of his time in the company of two horses of the finest Arabian breed, to whom he related his singular adventures, and discoursed with them on the exalted nature, the noble virtues of their happy kindred in the Southern Ocean. The only human beings whose occasional presence he could tolerate were his second son and his wife, my grandfather and grandmother, who imbibed his lofty views and pure morality, and learned from him to speak the Houyhnhnm language. Both my grandfather and my father often expressed a wish to visit this island, but received no encouragement from the great traveller, who remembered with keen anguish his own expulsion from this land.

"'I do not wish, my son,' he said, 'that you should endure the agony of mind which I experienced when I became an outcast from that paradise.'

"My father took the surname of Hippophil (horse-lover), and I was christened Philip.

Revolt of the Horses

"Brought up as I was in a Houyhnhnm atmosphere, and with a knowledge of the Houyhnhnm language, it was not unnatural that I should inherit my father's views and his longing to search for the better land; but I had to restrain the impulse out of deference to his wishes. His early death, however, quickly followed by that of my mother and my grandparents, left me without a tie of duty to bind me to my country. I inherited considerable wealth, and was, therefore, able to follow the inclination of my heart, which urged me to follow in my great ancestor's footsteps, in spite of all his warnings. I may mention here that, like my predecessor, I had a preference for a vegetable diet, and found no difficulty in sustaining my own life without destroying that of my fellow-creatures.

"In pursuance of my difficult quest, therefore, I embarked a few months ago on the ship *Mongolia*, bound for the Cape of Good Hope. I took with me the horse who now stands beside me and who, however insignificant he may appear in this august assembly, was the noblest creature with whom I had come in contact. As this island appears in no chart, and is only known to the world from the autobiography of my great grandfather, the chance of reaching it seemed extremely small. I only knew that he was on the voyage from the Cape of Good Hope to Van Diemen's Land when the mutiny broke out, which ended in his exposure on what seemed to the sailors an uninhabited island. At the Cape I

Revolt of the Horses

found a vessel bound for Australia, on which I secured a passage, trusting to my instinct to recognise this land, should we gain sight of it on our way. On the second day, we were driven due south by a furious gale from the north, and laboured for three days and nights in a terrific sea. The sailors, worn out by incessant toil and sleeplessness, at last abandoned the helm, over-powered the ship's officers, broke into the spirit stores, and sought oblivion in drunkenness. A few of the passengers, with some sailors whom they bribed, secretly lowered a boat and left the vessel, but probably perished on the waters. I saw them too late, just as they were pushing off. They were also seen by a woman, who, with a child in her arms, rushed wildly to the side of the vessel and piteously entreated them at any rate to save her child. As they remained deaf to her entreaties, she tried to jump into the boat, missed it, and was no more seen. On the fourth day we struck a hidden rock at the time of high tide. My equine companion and myself, the only sober beings on board, endeavoured to reach the land by swimming, and, as you know, were washed up on your shores in an apparently life-less state. All the rest fell a prey to the roaring sea."

CHAPTER II

THE foregoing narrative, though delivered with an accent which made it difficult to the Houyhnhnms to understand it, was listened to with breathless interest to the end. At its conclusion, a low whinny arose from the audience, followed by a deep silence, which was at last broken by the King himself.

"You have witnessed," he began, "the strange, almost miraculous spectacle of a Yahoo speaking our tongue, though uncouthly, and uttering thoughts which bespeak a certain amount of intelligence. Many of the things he speaks of, and the words he uses, are unknown to us; but enough is clear. Now, can we trust the statements of so false and cunning a creature as we know the Yahoo to be?"

No sooner had he uttered these words than a loud neighing was heard from the outskirts of the crowd, which directed all attention to that quarter. The sound proceeded from a magnificent Houyhnhnm, of unusual size and beauty, who was endeavouring to make his way to the dais, and for whom, as soon as his intentions were seen, a passage was made by the others with every mark of affection and respect. Having reached the immediate presence

Revolt of the Horses

of the King, he bent his grand head by way of salute, and placing his off fore foot gently on the shoulder of the astonished Hippophil, began as follows :—

"Nothing can be more natural, O King, than your distrust of all that comes from a creature bearing so base a form as this. But I am able of my own certain knowledge to confirm the truth of all that he has said ; for it was my great-grand-father who received his great-grandfather, and in my early years I have often heard my grand-father speak of the intelligent, docile, and amiable Yahoo who was by accident cast upon our shores. So great, he told me, was the progress he made in wisdom and virtue that he overcame, to a certain extent, his father's natural disgust for his form ; and he would gladly have kept him here, but yielded, of course, to the general wish that Hippophil should depart. How complete the reformation of his vile Yahoo nature was, we may gather from the tale of his descendant, who has evidently imbibed his spirit and inherited his virtues. My great-grandfather took much plea-sure in conversing with the first Gulliver, and hearing his descriptions of the extraordinary race of half-reasonable Yahoos from which he sprang. One of his statements, however, was received with insurmountable incredulity—viz. that in the far-off country from which he came the Yahoos ruled, and millions of Houyhnhnms were subject to their will. But even this inconceivable and horrible state of things receives some confirmation from the

Revolt of the Horses

poor creature before us, and his apparently subordinate relation to this Yahoo."

During this address, Hippophil became deeply affected, and at last, in a paroxysm of joy and gratitude at having found a friend in that strange assembly, he fell on his knees and kissed the hoofs of his generous advocate.

Meanwhile, the thoroughbred horse, lost in amazement and confusion of mind at all that he saw and heard around him, stood trembling under a sense of bewilderment and humiliation. At last he sank to the ground, and crouched low at the feet of the King, who regarded him with mingled curiosity and compassion, and then addressed him.

" Oh, thou unfortunate—shall I call thee Houyhnhnm?—can this be true? Art thou in that still glorious form — though scarred and sullied, and robbed of its full nobility and grace—art thou and thy fellows in that dark, strange land of contradictions, in deed and in truth subject to creatures in that vile shape?" (pointing to Hippophil).

The thoroughbred groaned, and hesitated to proclaim his shame.

" If thou art in any degree a Houyhnhnm," continued the King, "thou canst not lie."

The poor horse, trembling and breaking out into a violent sweat, breathed forth a " Yes," which, though faint as a sigh, was heard, in the dead silence of painful expectation, in every part of the vast hall. Then, however, loud indignant neighing and snorting, accompanied by trampling of feet,

18

Revolt of the Horses

resounded on all sides, and especially from the younger and the female Houyhnhnms. An almost threatening movement took place in the direction of the unhappy Hippophil, who was, however, protected from the first rush by the person and authority of his protector, Pegasus. The King himself, raising his stately head, swept the assembly with his large and lustrous eyes, and the murmurs instantly subsided and the tumult ceased.

"We are Houyhnhnms," he said; "we do not punish this poor wretch for the sins of his whole race."

Hippophil knelt before the dais, and raised his hands in supplication.

"What think ye," added the monarch; "what shall we do with these waifs of the sea—this—Houyhnhmn?—and this Yahoo?"

All were silent for a few minutes, when their friend Pegasus answered and said:

"An opportunity is now afforded us of enlarging the knowledge we gained from the first Gulliver, and which has become hereditary in my family. In our further investigations we shall derive inestimable assistance from the 'horse' as he is called. From the testimony of these two, whose statements will supplement and control each other, we shall be enabled fully to penetrate the dark mystery which the first Hippophil only partially revealed. And if," he added in a higher key, and with a certain amount of excitement, "if, as the first Gulliver declared, it be indeed true that myriads of our kinsmen are held in degrading

Revolt of the Horses

bondage in lands beyond the sea; if they are imprisoned, mutilated, scourged, put to tasks beyond their strength; if they have been robbed of their beauty and intelligence by centuries of degrading bondage, then it will be for us to consider what measures should be taken to emancipate them from oppression, and to exterminate the foul race whose footsteps seem ever marked by tears and blood. I cannot," he added more quietly, "ask anyone else to harbour this poor Yahoo; but I have a hereditary regard for him, and will provide for him myself. It would hurt my feelings, as well as his, were I to send him to the kennels of our own filthy slaves, who would certainly kill him. I will, therefore, if no objection is raised, place him and his companion in a shed not far from my own house, and provide him with corn and fruits—for, as you have heard, he abhors the bloody banquets of his kind. By this arrangement no one will be annoyed by his presence, and I can summon him at any time when I wish to discourse with him, and produce him before any future assembly."

The King bowed a gracious assent, and all present neighed approval. They then streamed forth from the building, discussing the marvels they had heard, and the weighty import of the words of Pegasus.

And now in all directions might be seen a spectacle of which even an English race or fox-hunt can give but a faint idea. The younger Houyhnhnms galloped side by side in friendly

Revolt of the Horses

emulation, and with ever-increasing speed, over hill and plain, their whole frames quivering with delight, their long manes floating in the breeze. The rocks and valleys re-echoed their loud neighing, and filled the air with sounds of joy and triumph. The more advanced in age trotted quietly to some eminence, which afforded a goodly prospect over the grassy plains, the fragrant groves, and the azure sea ; while around them frisked and gambolled the young colts and fillies, with endless contortions of their little bodies, expressive of the delicious sense of freedom, and the spontaneous joy of early childhood. In the far distance might be seen groups of filthy Yahoos, who retired with loud chattering and mutual recrimination on the approach of their masters, and endeavoured to conceal their hated forms. Not so far away, and quietly feeding, might also be seen a number of asses, which were often employed in preference to Yahoos, as being more cleanly and amiable, for any work which seemed suited to their powers.

Meantime, Pegasus, true to his word, had conducted Hippophil and the horse to a kind of shed or stable, charmingly situated beneath a spreading oak by the side of a crystal stream. Hippophil was able to furnish this abode with several articles of human furniture—tables, chairs, and chests of clothes—which had been washed up from the broken vessel. Like his ancestor he managed to grind his oats between flat stones and to prepare a sort of Scotch oatmeal, which, with vegetables and delicious fruit of every kind, was sufficient for his wants. He might, indeed, have caught the ground game, for the hares and rabbits played about his path, and the birds showed no signs of fear at his approach; but he knew that the use of such food would tend to lower him in the eyes of his kind patrons.

Hippophil was now supremely happy in having, by an almost miraculous combination of circumstances, found the land of which he had dreamed from his very infancy, and seen with his own eyes the godlike beings among whom it was the dearest wish of his heart to live and die. He had heard so much of their appearance, character and mode of life, that he now, for the first time, felt himself at home, freed at once from the heavy load of anxiety and fear which weighs on every son of man. Yet, occupied as he was in contemplating the grand forms of his revered masters, he did not forget or neglect the poor thoroughbred, who remained in the same state of depression and self-abasement, and rarely ventured to leave the shed. Hippophil, too, avoided frequent contact both with Houyhnhnms and Yahoos, fearing by his presence to offend the delicate senses of the former, or to draw on himself the malignant attention of the latter. His chief hope of intercourse with the higher intelligences by which he was surrounded lay in the favour shown him at the assembly by Pegasus, and in this he was not disappointed. His distinguished patron cherished a very lively remembrance of the tradition of his great-grandfather's conversa-

Revolt of the Horses

tions with the first Gulliver, and had even learned a little English from him, which he delighted to employ in his intercourse with his client. He was especially desirous of gaining a clear insight into the character of the strange, semi-reasonable animals whom Hippophil represented, and to learn in what respects, and to what extent, they differed from the loathsome Yahoos, whom in appearance they so closely resembled. There were still many problems left unsolved by the tradition of the first Gulliver's statements. An intelligent, docile Yahoo, capable of admiring, and, in a humble way, of imitating the sublime virtues of his own nation, seemed to him a contradiction in terms. A no less interesting subject was the nature of the poor thoroughbred, who seemed to be a fallen Houyhnhnm, while Hippophil might be regarded as an exalted Yahoo. Pegasus regarded his poor kinsman with keen interest but evident pain. He endeavoured, however, by condescension and kindness to set him at his ease, and encouraged him to relate his experiences, and to explain his deep fall from the intellectual and spiritual perfection of his nobler kinsmen.

On one occasion, when Pegasus entered the dwelling of Hippophil, he was accompanied by a young Houyhnhnm of surpassing beauty, whose skin shone like the finest, softest velvet, and whose silken hair flowed in waving folds over his muscular but beautifully modelled neck. His large dark eyes, in which no white was seen, beamed with high spirit and intelligence; and his widely distended and flexible nostrils inhaled the air, as if the mere act of breathing were a delight. No words can express the beauty of his harmonious proportions, or do justice to the mingled strength and elasticity of his finely turned limbs. Awe-struck by the majestic presence of the royal scion, for as such he recognised him by the white star in his forehead, Hippophil sank on his knees, and the thorough-bred retreated into the background and turned away his head, hoping to escape notice. The Prince, for it was no other than the King's son, Aethon, who has been mentioned above, kindly motioned to Hippophil to rise, and reclining with Pegasus on some fresh hay, expressed a wish to hear what he had to say about his own land and nation. Pegasus recommended him to place himself at some distance from the Prince, whose nerves were rather sensitive, and who was unused to find himslf in the same room with a Yahoo. It was some time before Hippophil could nerve himself to speak, but he was greatly encouraged by the presence of his patron, and by Aethon's gracious manner.

"I must begin," he said at length, "by craving your indulgence for the imperfection of my speech. I must further and more especially beg, that if I seem to exalt unduly the race to which I belong, you will pardon me. You may trust me," he added, laying his hand on his heart, "to speak the simple truth, for in sympathy, at least,

Revolt of the Horses

I am a Houyhnhnm, and heartily despise the falsehood and meanness of my fellow-men. I have lived in almost entire separation from them, and they have regarded me as a visionary and a madman. All my hopes are centred here.

"But vile as we now are, but little raised above the Yahoos of this land, there is good reason to believe that it was not always so with us. Tradition and written records combine to prove that this now degraded form of ours was fashioned by the same Almighty being whom you worship, and was endowed by Him with a lofty intelligence and a pure and guileless heart. Our first parents were placed in a garden called Eden, similar in all respects to this blessed land; they lived on the fruits of the earth, guiltless of blood, in perfect happiness, in close and constant communion with their Creator. You will smile when you look at me and hear that they were godlike in form, and of perfect grace and beauty. Like you, they were free from disease and pain; like you they were nude, and so far from suffering inconvenience from the climate, every change in the atmosphere only brought a new sensation of delight — so harmoniously did their nature blend with that of the universe of which they formed a part. The lower animals around them saw in them only protectors and friends, and contributed by the infinite variety of their form and colour, their joyous movements and enchanting songs, to the amusement and delight of their beloved master—man. They were, in fact, what

Revolt of the Horses

you are in almost all respects, except that of form; and since I have been among you I have learned to understand the condition and character of our first parents, as described in our most ancient records.

"But soon a change occurred, which I find extremely difficult to describe to you in your own language. You will perhaps understand me when I say that what we call SIN changed man from a Houyhnhnm to a Yahoo, darkened his intellect, dulled his senses, degraded his outward form, substituted lust for love, and mutual hatred for mutual affection. External nature, too, underwent a corresponding change as if affected by the poison of sin. The sun, instead of only blessing man with warmth and light, now scorched his skin, blinded his eyes, and burnt up the ground which had hitherto spontaneously supplied his wants. The seasons changed, and his miserable body was tortured by the alternation of exhausting heat and benumbing frost. The lower animals, his once happy and confiding playmates, became the objects of his ruthless tyranny. He delighted in their slaughter, and even devoured their flesh, which he snatched in the short interval between death and corruption. His heart became the den of evil passions and unnatural appetites; the springs of benevolence dried up, and universal selfishness took the place of universal love. No one regarded his fellow, unless he could make him subservient to his pride or lust. Disease, hitherto unknown, brought on by excess and the brutality of the seasons, tortured his nerves and subjected him to periods of lingering misery and to early death—death, which, instead of being regarded as the birth-throe of still happier life in still more intimate communion with God, was feared and abhorred as even worse than life itself. The ground, being cursed for his sake, brought forth but little spontaneously, and could only be made to yield him sufficient food by continual and exhausting labour. The stronger made slaves of the weaker and refused to perform their share of the hateful work. They demanded that others should procure for them, not only the means of existence, but the baneful luxuries which enhanced the evils under which they groaned. The once glorious form of man became for the most part disgusting to the sight. Only in a few, and for the short period of childhood and youth, was there any resemblance to the happy pair which once wandered through the Garden of Eden. Conscious of their own deformity they concealed their wasted and discoloured bodies from the eyes of their fellowmen, by wearing the skin of some less hideous animal."

Hippophil here paused, and marked with pain the surprise and loathing expressed in the faces and gestures of his hearers. After a short silence, Pegasus asked permission of the Prince to put a few questions to Hippophil, suggested by what he had heard from his own grandfather.

Revolt of the Horses

"Your ancestor," he began, "on his first arrival among us, used to tell wondrous things of the 'science' and manual skill of his countrymen. Amongst other proofs of these gifts he instanced the wonderful machine in which he traversed the sea, which he said was propelled by the action of the winds. I suppose you came hither in the same way?"

"The vessel which brought me to your shores," replied Hippophil, "was of a far more perfect kind, and was moved, not by the uncertain and fitful force of the breezes, but by a newly-discovered agent called 'steam,' produced by the action of fire on water, which enables us to defy the force of contrary winds and to regulate our speed at will."

"What is fire?" said the Prince.

"Fire," replied Hippophil, "has the same effect of producing warmth as the sun. It would be of no use to you who know no unpleasant degree of cold, and do not cook your food; but our very existence depends on it, as we so seldom see or feel the sun. When applied to water it transforms it into floating vapour like the clouds; and when this is confined within narrow limits, it exerts a tremendous force in its struggles to be free. By controlling and regulating this force," added Hippophil, with something like an emotion of pride, "we can propel—almost as rapidly as a Houyhnhnm can gallop—enormous vessels of iron capable of containing several thousand men."

Revolt of the Horses

"But why," asked Pegasus, "do men wish to crowd together in a dark house tossed about by the winds and waves, when they might enjoy the green fields and the woods at home?"

Hippophil hesitated. At last he said in a low and depressed tone: "It is necessary in times of war, of which you have heard, no doubt, to send great ships to destroy the floating houses of other nations."

The Prince shuddered. At the request of Pegasus, Hippophil then explained to them the nature and effects of gunpowder, and the important part it had played in the modern history of mankind. He also spoke of the great advances which had been made in recent times, and of the still more remarkable results to be looked for from the discovery of dynamite, by which a single individual was enabled to blow up a whole street, and destroy hundreds of men in a moment.

"I understand," said the Prince, with flashing eyes; "this 'science' of which you boast is principally employed in the work of annihilation." Turning to Pegasus, he added: "All the tendencies of these 'men' seem to be the same as those of our own Yahoos; the grand object of both is the destruction of life, which the latter pursue with. teeth and nails, and the former with fire and sword." Then, rising from his recumbent posture, he prepared to go away, saying to Hippophil: "There is so much in your narrative that is so enigmatical, painful, and disgusting that I must break off this conference and take time for reflec-

29

Revolt of the Horses

tion—time to cleanse my mind from the foul and monstrous images which you have called up, which make me feel as if I had lost an hour in the company of Yahoos. I do not mean," he added kindly, as he saw Hippophil wince and blush at these words, "to hurt your feelings. I know how thoroughly your ancestor appreciated us, and how earnestly you, with your feeble powers, have striven to cast off the slough of your Yahoo nature. I shall not be deterred from hearing you again; but enough for to-day. Come, Pegasus, let us take a gallop on the shore, and forget, if we can, all the horrors we have heard." With a slight shake of the head to Hippophil, and a glance of compassion at Bend'or, who remained motionless at the other end of the shed, the noble pair departed at full speed towards the beach.

CHAPTER III

HIPPOPHIL, too, went forth into the fresh, clear air, redolent of sweet odours and vibrating to the joyous melody of birds, and gave himself up to the delicious sensations which thrilled his nerves and gladdened his heart. An ineffable peace entered into his soul as he wandered on and on through the delicious land, without a thought of time or place, until he came to a natural arbour not far from the strand, formed by the mingled branches and foliage of myrtle and orange trees. A bed of soft moss tempted him to rest awhile from his walk, and he sank into a rapturous reverie, floating, as it were, between earth and heaven. From this blissful state he was rudely awakened by the sound of voices in the immediate neighbourhood, which at once dispelled his visions, and called him back to the coarse, miserable world from which he had so lately escaped. Straining his attention to the utmost he heard, with a surprise and horror which no words can describe, not the gentle neighing of the noble Houyhnhnm, nor the shrill chatter of the Yahoo, but words of his own English tongue, from voices which he recognised as those of his fellow-passengers in the ill-fated *Mongolia*. While in the ship, Hippophil had overheard one of them, who went by the name

Revolt of the Horses

of Billy Stubbs, relating his escape from the course at Epsom, where he had been unjustly, he said, chased by the mob as a welsher, and had thought it prudent to leave his country for awhile. The other was an adventurer, who got up sham reports of gold and other mines at the Cape of Good Hope, and was now on his way to Australia with the money of the deluded shareholders. His name, or assumed name, was Eustace Delaroche, which stood him in good stead with some of his female clients. Both these worthies were dressed in the well-known style of the flash gentry, and still wore red ties, the worse for salt water, and gorgeous rings and shirt studs.

"Devilish lucky," said Stubbs, "that we stowed away some grub before the vessel drowned herself, for I see nothing in the shape of food in this queer place, except fruit, and that don't suit my inside."

"Nor mine neither," growled Delaroche. "But after all there must be men of some sort here, for there are fields of oats, and I see something like a stable there in the distance. We'd better lie close, for devil knows what sorts of brutes may turn up at any moment. I fancy I saw a big white monkey up a tree as we came along; but there *must* be men, and if they find our boat we shall be up a tree too."

"What a squeak we had for it!" said Stubbs. "Lucky we didn't wait for that blessed woman with the babby, who tried to jump into the boat —silly fool! She squealed so that I thought you were going to turn soft."

32

Revolt of the Horses

" Not I," said Delaroche, " but what rum critters them women is ; she didn't seem to care a blast about herself, only that blessed babby. However, every man for himself, say I, and devil take the hindmost. We weren't going to lose our chance, and I expect we're the only lucky ones."

" Lucky ! " said Stubbs. " Don't halloa till you're out of the wood. How are we to get away from this d——d hole. I'm sick of salt water, yah ! I've swallowed a hogshead, and don't at all like the thought of taking to the boat again without chart or compass—but what else is there in it ? "

" Hullo ! what's the row ? "

" Row," cried Stubbs, who had hastily risen to his feet with every mark of the greatest astonishment, and was peering through a narrow gap in the branches behind which they were hidden. " Look there ! " and he pointed to a meadow of oval form and vast extent round which a number of young Houyhnhnms were chasing one another, at a speed which no racer ever attained, while others came bounding through the surrounding thickets. " Look at that filly ! " said Stubbs, in a perfect paroxysm of surprise and admiration. " There's a head for you ! What a skin ! What a shoulder ! ! What legs ! ! ! "

His companion was equally astonished, and exclaimed, as the Houyhnhnms again passed within easy sight of their hiding-place : " What

Revolt of the Horses

a pace! D——n me if they couldn't give the best horse in England a hundred yards and beat him hollow. I wonder what heavy swell owns these beauties! Not a man to be seen!"

" I should like," said Stubbs, " to see the stud-groom ; I think I could give him a wrinkle. What wouldn't I give to put a pigskin on that filly, with a good bit in her mouth, and a pair of spurs. I'd take that frisk out of her pretty soon. I'd tame her, by G——! Why, I'd rather have a couple of them spankers in England than all the beastly old mines you ever lied about. I'd walk into the knowing ones."

The worthy pair continued to express their astonishment and delight in a jargon which was often unintelligible to Hippophil, garnished, as it was, with an astounding wealth and variety of blasphemous and filthy epithets, in which they strove to give vent to their excitement.

Hippophil meanwhile lay almost paralysed with terror, revolving in his mind what course to take. Should he allow these ruffians to be found by his Houyhnhnm protectors and be obliged to acknowledge them as his countrymen? Should he accost them and beg them to leave the island without being seen? Both courses seemed fraught with ruin. At last he stole from his retreat with every precaution against being seen, and, hastening to the abode of Pegasus, related to him the embarrassing occurrence, and besought him not to mention it to the other

34

Revolt of the Horses

Houyhnhnms, who might less quickly grasp the situation. Pegasus heard him with indulgence, and bidding him follow as quickly as he could galloped off in the direction of a camp of Yahoos. He addressed them in a few energetic words of command, and pointed with his off fore leg in the direction of the thicket in which the two men lay concealed. No sooner had the Yahoos, numbering some thirty or forty, caught his meaning than with a howl of delight they bounded forth in a troop towards the indicated spot. From a slight eminence Hippophil caught sight of Stubbs and Delaroche as they issued from their lair and ran at full speed towards the shore. The fearful yells of the Yahoos had warned them of their danger and they got a considerable start, which was, however, diminished at every moment. Hippophil followed to see the issue, without, of course, any idea of saving the wretched fugitives. As they neared the boat the Yahoos were only some fifty yards behind them. Stubbs, the bolder of the two, turned round and discharged his revolver at the foremost pursuer, who fell with a fearful shriek, mortally wounded. The others paused for a moment, thunderstruck with astonishment at the miraculous spectacle. At the same time Delaroche, whom terror had blinded, stumbled over the root of a tree and sprained his ankle.

"Come on, you fool!" shrieked Stubbs as his companion fell.

"Help me," cried Delaroche—" I've hurt my leg."

Revolt of the Horses

"Oh, d——n your beastly leg! What an idiot you must be—come on—how do you suppose I can get the boat off alone?"

Delaroche struggled on in the greatest pain and tumbled into the boat just as the Yahoos, recovering from their consternation, were within a few yards of them. Stubbs pushed off in the nick of time, while the disappointed herd of pursuers hurled big stones at them, and one, more adventurous than the rest, swam to the boat and climbed into it. A fierce scuffle ensued between Stubbs and the Yahoo. The latter used teeth and claws with some effect, but he was soon disabled by the stab of a long knife, and hurled back into the sea. Shaking his fist at the other Yahoos, Stubbs roared out:

"Yah! you wait till we come again, my hearties."

A favourable wind bore the two scamps, too villainous for drowning, away in the direction of a vessel which appeared to Hippophil like a speck on the horizon. Hippophil had only too good reason to know in the sequel that they escaped with their lives.

The Yahoos, with frantic cries of rage, bore away the bodies of their dead into the woods, and were soon lost to sight though not to hearing. Hippophil once more sought out Pegasus, and expressed his gratitude for his timely and effectual aid. He heard with great interest and some apprehension that another assembly had been called for the morrow to examine the thoroughbred, Bend'or, concerning his own per-

Revolt of the Horses

sonal history and the real state of others of his kind in the country from which he came. The tradition of the first Gulliver's account of the treatment to which horses—whom the Houyhnhnms regard as their own kindred—were subjected, seemed too strange and impossible for belief.

"They will expect you," said Pegasus, "to be present with Bend'or, and to help the latter to elucidate the truth. My evidence in your favour, and the traditional good opinion entertained of your ancestor, incline them to believe that you have overcome the natural Yahoo tendency to falsehood." On the morrow accordingly, in obedience to a working Houyhnhnm, Hippophil and Bend'or repaired to a basin, or natural amphitheatre, shut in by forest trees and fragrant shrubs, the meeting being too large to be accommodated in any building. On a small mound in the centre of the valley were the King, his royal consort, Leucippe, the young Prince Aethon and a royal filly about nine months old, whose graceful and delicate proportions contrasted charmingly with the noble and stately forms of her male kindred. Hippophil and the thoroughbred were placed at the foot of the mound, in front of the royal party. Bend'or, knowing the object of the meeting, was in a state of pitiable nervousness and terror, which was, however, somewhat relieved by the kind manner in which the King addressed him.

"Fear nothing," he said, "you are of our blood and race; and though the glory of your high

Revolt of the Horses

lineage has been dimmed by centuries of bondage,
we feel for you nothing but compassion. Strange,
almost incredible accounts have reached us of your
position in that distant land, and we wish to know
the truth—the *whole* truth, however revolting ; and
we hope that your enforced slavery to inferior
animals has not so far corrupted your nature as
to tempt you to say the thing which is not."

Encouraged by these words, delivered in a
gentle tone, Bend'or overcame his feeling of
humility and shame, and amidst the deep silence
of the crowded assembly made the following
statement :—

"My case is a peculiar one, and does not
adequately represent that of the great mass of
suffering creatures who pine and perish under
the tyranny of man. I lived in England, the
country most famous for its breed of horses,
whose people are considered the least cruel in
their treatment of what they call the lower
animals. (Here there was a slight neigh of
surprise and amazement from the younger
Houyhnhnms.) I belong to the *élite* of our
race, and am directly descended from the famous
Darley Arabian ; so that my veins are filled
with the noblest blood. My memory easily
carries me back to the first days of my life, for
I am but eight years old. I first saw the light
in a large stable in Newmarket, where I and
my poor mother, who afterwards dropped dead
in the streets of London from over-work, were
comfortably lodged. We were carefully tended,

Revolt of the Horses

protected from the cold, fed on the finest corn and hay, and led forth for gentle exercise on soft turf, on which I gambolled beside my mother till she was taken from me. When I had attained my full size, the comparative ease and freedom I had enjoyed were suddenly contracted, and I was what they call 'put into training,' and taught to move my legs in a certain way—to walk and trot and gallop. Bars of wood were placed across my back, a rope was fastened to my head, and I was made to run round and round in a circle. One day a leathern seat was fastened tightly on my back, a large bar of iron forced into my mouth, and suddenly, before I could prevent it, a man leaped on to my back. Wild with terror I sprang into the air and tried to shake him off. Finding all my efforts vain I rolled on the ground, severely hurting myself, but crushing my tormentor, who was borne off by his companions bruised and bleeding. The same attempt was made soon afterwards, and I again disposed of my rider by carrying him at full speed under the low branches of a tree. I was then chained to a heavy carriage and subjected to blows, from which there was no escape. Worn out and dispirited, seeing that all my resistance only resulted in heavier bondage and harder treatment, I yielded at last, and suffered myself to be mounted and directed by a choking iron in my mouth. I was then caressed and made much of, and continually visited by a man before whom my attendants

Revolt of the Horses

bowed low, and who watched my paces and calculated my strength and speed. I was often made to run side by side with other horses very like myself. One day, when I was about two years old, I was conveyed in a large box to a considerable distance from home and placed in another stable. A few days after I was led to a large plain in which many thousand men were assembled, shouting and rushing about in mad excitement. Here I met about a dozen other horses of the same age as myself, from whom, however, I could obtain no information respecting the purpose for which we had been brought together. We were not long left in uncertainty. After being ranged in an even line, we were urged into a quick gallop by our riders, who were all arrayed in bright colours, each of whom sought to make his horse run faster than the others. A spirit of rivalry seized me, and, moreover, I was tortured to the wildest excitement by stabs from a sharp iron in my rider's heel. Finding myself alongside of another horse of like speed to my own, I did my best to pass him, and with immense exertion succeeded in getting my head in front of his. As we passed a certain post, I heard my name repeated by thousands of spectators, who gesticulated and vociferated, threw their hats into the air, and comported themselves like madmen. I was then led into an enclosed space and surrounded by people, who patted me on the back and neck, stroked my nose, and passed their hands down

my reeking legs and bleeding sides. Some of
my admirers, called 'ladies,' laid their little hands
caressingly on my neck, as if conferring a favour
and an honour. Exhausted by my exertions,
trembling in every limb with excitement and
pain, and sickened by the heat and steam of the
crowd, I was led back to my stable, the silence
and darkness of which were a relief to my weary
limbs and jaded senses. These scenes were
repeated during some years of my life, but this
was my only triumph, because the only one in
which I had taken any interest. My spirit once
more revolted against the cutting whip and
lacerating spur, by which they sought to goad
me to victory. As my speed and docility diminished, a new career less full of pain, but even
more humiliating, was opened to me. Cooped
in a stall and highly fed I was forced into unnatural union with females of a lower grade, who
resembled, but oh! how inferior, the working
Houyhnhnms of this blessed land. Even for
these base uses I was soon unfit, and was then
transferred to a dark and filthy dungeon in
London, condemned to drag a carriage through
the streets, crowded with miserable creatures like
myself, and lashed into exertion beyond my
strength. One day I fell beneath my burden,
and was immediately surrounded by a gaping
crowd, some of whom helped the wretch who
drove me to beat me into rising. But there was
one among them—he who now stands by my
side—who loves and honours our race, even in

Revolt of the Horses

its degradation. Stepping boldly forward he rebuked my driver for his cruelty, purchased me for a small sum, and conveyed me into the country. There, freed from labour, I lived in close intercourse and mutual affection with my generous deliverer. From him I heard of the adventure of his great-grandfather, and his own longing desire to visit this delicious land — a desire which, as you know, has, by the favour of God, been happily fulfilled."

As Bend'or ended his tale, which was followed with breathless interest by the whole assembly, a loud murmur of excitement and indignation was heard from all sides. Even the King himself, usually so calm and stately, seemed strangely moved; fire seemed to breathe from his widely distended nostrils, and flash from his large full eyes, while the veins in his neck swelled almost to bursting. Still more excited was the young Prince Aethon, who, unable to endure the thought of the woes and indignities to which millions of his kinsmen were subjected by a Yahoo race, galloped away to the nearest river, and, plunging into it, sought to assuage the unwonted fever of wrath which boiled in his veins. The recital of the horse had a marked effect, too, in turning the attention of the audience to Hippophil, whose conduct roused their highest admiration. Crowding round him, they so far overcame their repugnance to his Yahoo form, that many a noble hoof was raised to rest gently on his shoulder, or stroke his face; many a muzzle even touched

Revolt of the Horses

his cheek in kindness, and neighings of admiration were heard on every side. Hippophil could only respond to this unlooked-for outburst of good feeling towards himself by tears of gratitude and joy. But now a movement of the King's head produces immediate silence and attention. Mastering his emotion he spoke as follows :—

"Houyhnhnms! ye have heard the sad tale of this poor outcast of our holy and mighty brotherhood. I *know* that his words are true. This is not the time to come to any resolution. At the present moment we are unfit for calm deliberation or wise resolve. I will reflect on what we have heard. I will project my mind into every quarter from which knowledge on the subject may be obtained, and you shall know the conclusions at which I arrive. One thing only I will say at once; that no effort, no sacrifice were too great to save our brethren—transformed, degraded, yet our brethren—from the nameless tyranny under which they languish. Such a race as those more than Yahoos who live towards the setting sun is a blot on the fair face of Nature and deserves extermination. Farewell!—the assembly is dismissed."

His words were received with a whinny of sympathy, and the Houyhnhnms left the place with drooping heads, and, for the first time in their happy lives, with a feeling near akin to sorrow.

CHAPTER IV

NOTHING occurred for some time to break the even tenor of the happy life which Hippophil enjoyed in common with everyone about him. The only annoyance from which he suffered arose from the curiosity and malice of the Yahoos, who claimed him as one of themselves. On one occasion he was bathing in the river—far, as he thought, from every eye—when a troop of the noisome animals rushed into the water to seize him, while others carried off his clothes. Only the timely approach of some working horses on their rounds caused the Yahoos to decamp, leaving his clothes at a short distance from the river.

It was known, however, that the Inner Council had held several meetings in the King's presence, and that most of its members, and especially the young Prince Aethon, were in favour of immediate and energetic action in the shape of promoting a general revolt of the horses in England ; while others were said to think the enterprise too vast, and the results too uncertain to be ventured on without the fullest knowledge and the most careful preparation. Even this slight difference of opinion was something quite unusual, because reason and right feeling were universal, and always brought them in the end to the same result. Of course, the decision of the King was looked to as final and all-sufficient. The monarch often conversed with Bend'or, and heard further details of the condition of horses in England, which drove him more and more to the conclusion that some grand plan must be adopted to put a stop to the cruel tyranny under which they groaned.

We must now leave for a time the happy abode of the Houyhnhnm, in which peace and joy perennially reigned, and transfer our thoughts to Cape Town in the Cape of Good Hope. In a small smoking-room of the "British Hotel," at about midnight, four men sat drinking together, engaged in animated conversation. One of these, a man of about thirty-five years of age, was distinguished from the others by the unmistakable marks of the English "gentleman." No one who knew English society could for a moment suppose that Lord Salford was a professional or mercantile man, or that he had ever earned a single penny by the work of his hands or brains. Yet it would be difficult to say which of the numerous definitions of a gentleman he embodied, for he was clumsy in form and gait, slovenly in dress, coarse in his manners, ignorant in mind ; and every bad passion and unbridled desire had written their names large upon his face. But he was a "gentleman," and he knew it, and those who were with him knew it, and treated him accordingly. His career was one which has not unfrequently been run by "gentlemen." His father was the very model of the English nobleman—the highest type which modern civilisation has produced—sensible, upright, patriotic, kind and generous to his dependants, modest and genial among his equals, a tender husband, and an affectionate father. His darling object was to fit his only son for the high position in which he was to pass his life, by giving him a liberal education, and all the advantages of a well-ordered, happy home and the *best* society, in the true sense of the word. But like some noxious seed, sown and tended in a fair garden, he grew up to disappoint all his fond father's hopes. It seemed as if the evil nature of some far-off ancestor had taken possession of his body, and ruled without control in his heart and members; for from his earliest boyhood he stubbornly resisted every good influence, and resolutely set his face to do evil. "Advised to leave" Harrow, he went to Oxford, where he did what he could to corrupt others and disgrace himself. When he came of age his father made him a handsome allowance, which he exceeded tenfold, raising money by post-obits and every other device, and at last by selling his reversion of the entailed property. At his father's death he took advantage of a flaw in his will to get possession of the legacies to his sisters, with which he fled to the Continent and wandered about from one haunt of vice to another. He was now at Cape Town, with a few thousands still at his command, in the company of outlawed sharpers, adventurers, and blacklegs.

Revolt of the Horses

The second member of the quartette, Mr Walker, who looked about forty years of age, had a short, thick-set figure, reddish hair, a brick-dust complexion, a close-shaven face, and a frame of cast-iron and wire. He had been a saddler, but his love for racing, and its cognate pursuits and pleasures, had soon brought him to bankruptcy, and led him to look to bookmaking on the turf as a means of livelihood. A run of ill-luck had made it prudent for him to leave his country, and he now occupied the position of humble friend to Lord Salford, whom he addressed with a sulky deference, which savoured more of fear than respect. The other two were our old acquaintances, Stubbs and Delaroche, whose disastrous exit from Houyhnhnm-land we have described above. Lord Salford was stretched at full length on a horse-hair sofa, with a table before him, on which stood bottles of different spirituous liquors, a jug of hot water and glasses, and a box of cigars. Close to his chief sat Walker, the other two were opposite to him ; Lord Salford was listening with a partly-affected smile of derision to Stubbs' glowing account of what they had seen in the island on which they were shipwrecked.

"I give you my sacred word, my lord," said Stubbs, "that if we could but get hold of two or three of them spankers that me and Delaroche saw, we could sweep every racecourse and empty the pockets of every sportsman in England."

"Oh, of course," said Salford with a sneer, "if you give *your sacred word* for it, there is nothing

47

more to be said. Why, d——n you," he added, with a ferocious look at Stubbs, "I suppose you see some colour in my eye which you mistake for green, or you would not talk such blasted rot to *me!* I believe the whole thing is a plant of yours and Delly's there ; but it won't wash."

"Well," said the latter, "I don't wish to go against your lordship, but what Stubbs says is as true as the Gospel, and a good deal truer, according to the clever ones. We saw horses out there to which Eclipse, Flying Dutchman, Gladiateur, and Bend'or were fools and dray-horses—I can't help saying as I find."

"The thing sounds queer," said Walker, with some timidity of manner, "but if it *were* true, it would be a great find, and one might make a pot of money, no doubt."

"I see you all hang together like thieves as you are," said Lord Salford, who was really strongly impressed by what he heard ; "but you must get up very early, as the Bible says, before you can walk round me. I have seen one or two things in *my* life."

A dead silence followed, during which cigars were puffed, and brandies absorbed. After a long pause Lord Salford said, with an air of indifference ; "And supposing a man were ass enough to go into this thing, how would you propose to work it?"

"Oh!" said Stubbs eagerly, "the thing's as easy as pie. I know a couple of half-castes here who are no end with the lasso. We might get near them at night, and if the old 'uns were too wide

Revolt of the Horses

awake, we could always nobble some colts and fillies, which would suit our book first-rate. We should want a small vessel fitted up with horse-boxes, and a dozen smart fellows with revolvers to tackle those beastly white monkeys — who frightened old Delly so—and settle the owners of the horses, if there are any. We could easily lay hold of a few young horses before they came on us in any numbers."

"And who is to pay the shot?" said Lord Salford in a loud voice. "I don't suppose you could raise £5 among you, and I'll be d——d if you get it out of me." This sort of talk went on till dawn, the result being that Lord Salford, having secured to himself the lion's share in the horses to be captured by the others, without his personal aid—for though he was not deficient in courage, he hated all exertion—agreed to advance £300 for the purposes of the expedition.

Meantime our friends, the Houyhnhnms, were enjoying halcyon days in their lovely island. Bend'or was daily improving in appearance, and deriving fresh hope and courage from the friendly condescension with which he was treated. Hippophil, too, was now in the enjoyment of all that he had dreamed of, and would have been supremely happy could he have forgotten the intrusion of Stubbs and Delaroche, and divested himself of all fears of their return. An uneasy presentiment of evil often led him to the shore where their boat had been moored, and the adventurous Yahoo slain; and often, when night came on, he ascended the cliff and peered into the offing for the light of some distant vessel. Shame of his species made him unwilling to betray his fears publicly, and Bend'or was the only one who shared his anxieties and aided him in his watch. But should an attack in force be made, how could it be met? No dependence could be placed on the Yahoos, who would be dispersed by the first rifle shots, and how could he explain to the Houyhnhnms the deadly effect of the diabolical arms of precision, which would, of course, be worn by the invaders? Would they not advance with proud confidence against the "civilised" Yahoos and fall victims to their deadly aim? One thing, and one only, could he determine in his mind, and that was to encounter every danger, to meet captivity and even death, in the service of the noble beings to whom he owed all that he was and had.

One evening a little before nightfall, after having surveyed the part of the north coast where a landing might be most easily effected, he ascended the cliff which rose gradually towards the west, remembering that he had seen a practicable path which led down to the shore. No sooner had he reached the highest point of the rocks than, to his consternation and dismay, he saw the lights of a vessel about two miles off. At the same time the measured splash of oars struck his attentive ear, and by the fast fading twilight he could just discern three large boats, apparently filled with men. He heard a voice which seemed familiar to him shouting from the largest boat to the others:

Revolt of the Horses

"Why, we've missed the landing—this isn't the place where we touched at last time—what an infernal nuisance!" There was then silence for a time, till he heard the grinding noise of a keel as it struck the sands. Then another voice, "It's no use trying to find the right place in the dark—we're in for it now. There's a path up the cliff and we can get up there and turn in for the night. It's better than knocking about in the boats and being jolted to pieces." "Right you are," said another; "after all, we can't do anything till we have looked about us and seen how the land lies. Just hand out the rum and rifles in case of need, and let each man keep his revolver ready. We shan't want bed-clothes on a night like this, when the queen's baby might sleep out-of-doors. I see the moon rising, so we shall have light to choose our beds; by Jove, what a moon!" Hippophil then heard the sound of many feet ascending the cliff. A hundred plans in succession chased one another through his brain, but all seemed fraught with ruin, and he remained in a kind of stupor for a full hour, during which the marauders were engaged in choosing their bivouac and settling themselves for the night. At last he roused himself from his lethargy, and, despairing of direct resistance, he resolved to have recourse to stratagem, as affording the only hope of safety. Coming forth from his hiding-place he accosted Stubbs, as if delighted to see him. The moon had now risen with a refulgent splendour surpassing that of the Egyptian deserts, and no sooner was he recognised than a loud shout of astonishment rose

51

Revolt of the Horses

from the new comers: "Hallo! old fellow," cried Delaroche, "where the devil did you drop from? Why, we thought you had gone to glory months ago!" All gathered round him with eager curiosity and a thousand questions, and it was some time before he could get a hearing.

In a story of well-mingled truth and fiction he related how he had been thrown up on the shore with his thoroughbred. As he had found the island inhabited only by white and very savage apes and wild horses, he had with difficulty sustained life on some oats standing ripe in the fields, and on the shell-fish which he found on the shore.

"And nothing to drink?" said Stubbs. "Poor devil—take a pull," handing him his flask.

Hippophil complied, and in every possible way endeavoured to keep the rascals in good humour.

"What you say about the monkeys," continued Stubbs, "is quite true, for we have seen them —the chattering beasts had nearly done for us —but we'll pay them off. But how about the horses?—do you mean to say that no one owns them? That won't *quite* do, for better bred and better groomed animals I never saw; besides there are stables all over the place!"

"Perhaps Philly has annexed them all," said Walker; "if so, I'm afraid there'll be a coolness between him and us, for we mean to have some of the tidy nags of which Stubbs has told us."

"That's what we've come for," said the latter, turning to Hippophil, with a half-threatening

Revolt of the Horses

look, "and no mistake; and if you're going to help us, all the better for you; if not, you'll have to look out for squalls, that's all."

Hippophil again declared that he had seen no human being in the land, unless they reckoned the white apes, and expressed his willingness to aid them in their enterprise, if they would in return give him a passage home in their ship.

"Well, look here, old boy," said Stubbs, who, judging from himself, always suspected his friends of a desire to overreach him, "fine words butter no parsnips—and handsome is as handsome does. If you mean to run straight, I'll tell you what you shall do. You know your way about by this time, I should think. It's a fine night — and them monkeys and the horses will be gone to by - by. Just you show me the way to some of them stables we saw, and prove your words that there are no men about. I'll just take my little case of instruments with me, for fear of accidents, and a bridle and a pair of spurs, in case we come across something tidy in the way of horseflesh. We shall have to keep dark and not bring those cursed apes upon us."

We may imagine the horror with which Hippophil heard this proposal; and it was with difficulty that he mastered an insane desire to seize the ruffian by the throat. He ventured to suggest some reason for postponing their reconnoitre, but seeing that he only roused suspicion, he at last declared his readiness to accompany Stubbs, inwardly praying that he

53

Revolt of the Horses

might find some means of misleading him and frustrating his purpose.

"That's right, old fellow—we'll start at once; and the fewer the better; so Philly, you and I will go alone, and you other fellows stop here comfortably till we come back and tell you all about it." So saying, he stuck his revolver into his belt, thrust a large flask of brandy into his pocket, and tied a bridle loosely round his neck. "Now then, Philly, lead on to glory!"

The rest of the party were too much taken by surprise by the suddenness of the proposition to formulate the strong objection they felt to allowing Stubbs to take the matter into his own hands; and the pair moved rapidly off towards the interior of the island. When once out of sight and call of the marauders they moved quietly and cautiously, and stopped at every sound, for Hippophil was as anxious not to be seen in such company by the Houyhnhnms as Stubbs to escape the notice of the Yahoos. They stopped at every sound, and crouched low among the bushes. Nothing, however, was heard more formidable than the noise made by a hare startled from her form, or by a bird as it rustled through the brake, or poured forth its liquid passion from the tree. At any other time the balmy sweetness of the air, the bright soft moonlight, and the pensive melody of the nightingale, would have filled the soul of Hippophil with rapture; but he was tortured by the thought of the slender hold he had on all these pleasures;

54

and as for his companion, *he* would rather have been in a gin shop or a gambling-hell. After more than an hour's walking, during which Stubbs expressed, in curses not loud but deep, his impatience and displeasure at seeing no horses, they came to a belt of flowering shrubs —oleander, myrtle, and gum-cistus—surrounding a meadow of deep rich grass. In the centre of this field was a long low structure of pine wood and osier, through which the refreshing breezes passed with little interruption. The place was well known to Hippophil as the abode of a matron Houyhnhnm of the highest class, who occupied it with her two young ones, a colt and a filly. Hippophil endeavoured to avert the catastrophe, which he could not but foresee, by saying carelessly that the shed was unoccupied.

"We'll soon see that," said Stubbs, and, stealing softly through the open door, he entered the building. A flood of moonlight, hardly diminished by the open osier work which connected the upright supports of the roof, illumined the interior, and revealed to Stubbs what was to him the most glorious vision which had ever dazzled mortal eyes. Reclining on a bed of straw, with her forelegs stretched out before her, and her head bent down in deep sleep, lay a matron Houyhnhnm of the noblest form. On each side of her, with their pretty heads pressed close to her soft and lustrous neck, lay a colt and a filly, also fast asleep, but with their limbs continually twitching, as if, even in sleep, they were engaged

Revolt of the Horses

in their gambols on the grass. For once in his life, overpowered by his feelings, the ruffian left the building again and rejoined Hippophil, who, in mortal terror, had lingered on the threshold. Seizing his arm and hurrying him to a little distance, Stubbs poured forth a string of oaths and blasphemies, expressive of his astonishment and delight. "What a brood mare! What a colt! What a filly! £50,000 wouldn't buy them! There isn't a horse in the world that can hold a candle to them! I'm d——d if any living soul shall lay a finger on her," he added, turning fiercely upon Hippophil, "as long as I can draw a trigger." While thus speaking, he hastily let out the bridle he had brought with him, both in length and breadth, and passed silently into the building. Hippophil followed him, and to his utter consternation saw him pass the bridle over the mare's head without completely rousing her, and then, by a sudden and skilful jerk, force the bit into her mouth.

"Good heavens!" said Hippophil, "what are you doing?"

"I'll soon show you what I'm doing," rejoined Stubbs, and seizing the bridle, he kicked the matron in the side, saying, "Come up, old girl, and show us your paces."

As soon as the bewildered Houyhnhnm had risen to her feet, Stubbs leapt on to her back and urged her towards the entrance, in which Hippophil stood with extended arms, as if to bar his exit.

Revolt of the Horses

"Get out of that!" shrieked Stubbs, "or I'll ride over you, by G——!"

The unfortunate Houyhnhnm, still in a sort of trance—half sleep and half bewilderment—moved mechanically on until she was thoroughly aroused by the prick of the rider's spur. The dream became a terrible reality. She felt, with the utmost surprise and consternation, the iron in her mouth, and turning her long neck, she beheld the hideous form of a Yahoo firmly seated on her back. Maddened by disgust and terror, she leapt three times into the air, and as Stubbs still kept his seat, she rushed with the speed of the wind in the opposite direction of that in which the boats lay, and no efforts of Stubbs could stop or even check her course. Even in this extremity, a sentiment of admiration passed through his mind at the wonderful speed of his mount, and the stride with which she flew over the highest and broadest obstacles. After narrowly escaping destruction from the low hanging branches of the trees, he now emerged into an open plain. Peering into the distance by the full light of the moon, which shone like a milder sun, he thought he saw a sudden dip in the land before him. Bold as he was by nature and education, he could not but tremble at his position on an utterly uncontrollable animal, wild with terror, and, in all probability, with a ravine before him. In a sudden paroxysm of fear—for he dearly loved his foul life and its low and beastly pleasures—he tugged at the

Revolt of the Horses

bridle with all the force of his iron arms—in vain! Another minute and the ravine would be reached, and then! "There's nothing for it," he said to himself, grinding his teeth; and, drawing forth his revolver with his right hand, he discharged two shots into the noble creature's head, close to the right ear. Mortally wounded, she first stood straight up on her hind legs, and then, with a sudden change, threw her heels into the air with a frantic violence which no rider could resist, and flung her persecutor, like a bolt from a bow, against a sharp rock which jutted out of the ground at the very edge of the ravine. She then sank fainting to the ground.

Meantime Hippophil, who had been utterly powerless to prevent the catastrophe, was making his way with his utmost speed on the easily found track of the doomed steed and rider. In front of him were the little colt and filly, who, unable to keep pace with their mother, were following in her wake as fast as their little legs would carry them. No words can describe his grief and horror when he reached the spot where the noble matron was lying. On each side of her drooping head, and stained by the blood which flowed copiously from her wounds, lay the young Houyhnhnms, nestling in their accustomed posture. The poor mother, recovering for a moment from her swoon, was tenderly gazing on them with her large eyes, now clouded by approaching death. Her deep flanks heaved violently as she strove to draw her breath, choked by the blood which streamed

Revolt of the Horses

from her mouth; a shudder of disgust passed through her frame as she caught sight of the kneeling Hippophil. Regarding him with a look of lofty contempt, which cut him to the heart, she faintly murmured, "Yahoo!" Then touching the heads of her offspring with her mouth, she sank back with a groan and gave up the ghost.

Hippophil was heartbroken at the thought that he had been recognised and evidently regarded as an accomplice in the foul murder. But he still retained sufficient presence of mind to see that this was no time for the indulgence of grief, and that action—immediate action—alone could avert a recurrence of many such scenes of horror. The moon was still high, shining brightly on the mangled body of Stubbs, which Hippophil carried into the bushes and hid as well as he was able. Then, with all the speed he could command, he hurried back on his footsteps, and made for the habitation of Pegasus. Having roused the noble Houyhnhnm from his sleep, and begged for a private conference, he walked up and down with him at some distance from the dwelling, and told him of the landing of the marauders, and the terrible episode which he had just witnessed. Pegasus understood at once the position of affairs, for the infernal powers of the foreign Yahoos had been described to his great-grandfather by the first Gulliver. He therefore immediately saw the necessity and the wisdom of Hippophil's proposal —viz. that the Houyhnhnms should withdraw *en masse* to the interior of the island, and leave him

to devise some scheme for outwitting and destroying the rest of the marauders, who would no
longer have the advantage of Stubbs' ability and
daring. He saw that open force was useless
against their firearms—that their foul designs
could only be met by deceit and stratagem, of
which no Houyhnhnm was capable, and to which
no Houyhnhnm would condescend. Without a
moment's delay they went together to the King,
who, on hearing their report, issued orders for the
immediate retreat of the whole Houyhnhnm community to a well-known *rendezvous* about five
miles to the north, away from the coast. He also
sent a party of working horses to drive the whole
mass of Yahoos in the same direction. In less
than an hour the Houyhnhnms might be seen
bounding away under the moonlight, while a
select number superintended the removal of the
murdered matron, whose body was laid on hurdles
covered with soft moss, and borne along on the
shoulders of Yahoos in the wake of the retreating
army.

With a mind greatly relieved by their departure, Hippophil hurried to the spot where
he had hidden the body of Stubbs. He found
him still alive, but with his head battered in
a shocking manner. He was quite unconscious
of Hippophil's presence, and kept murmuring
almost unintelligibly in his delirium. The only
words which Hippophil could catch showed
that his mind was still occupied by the ruling
passion :

Revolt of the Horses

"Spanking brood mare—worth a king's ransom
—colt wins Derby easy—what's the odds?" A
dead silence followed, then the death rattle, and
all was over. Having removed his revolver,
Hippophil hastily carried the corpse to the edge
of the ravine, and hurled it into the depths below;
he then hastened back to the bivouac of the
marauders, which he reached as day was breaking.

The party, which consisted of Walker, Delaroche, several adventurers who had passed their
lives "in the bush," half-a-dozen men of colour
skilled with the lasso, and a few hangers-on of
the basest sort, rose eagerly from their recumbent posture as they saw Hippophil approaching, and boisterously demanded his news.

"What the hell has kept you so long? Where's
Stubbs? Seen any horses?—any natives?—any
of those beastly monkeys?"

"Do give a fellow time to take breath," said
Hippophil, assuming as much as possible the
tone of his company. "It's all right — Stubbs
is waiting out there till we pick him up—he has
hurt his foot against a stump. We've seen no
men, but some A1 horses; but they are too
quick for us. One big herd is gone off north
like a whirlwind. We must follow them—try
and steal on them at night with lassos — and
pick up colts and fillies. Some fellows should
go back to the ship and get prog and drink for
several days; and the boats should be brought
round to the old landing-place; we should never
get wild horses down the cliff."

Revolt of the Horses

"Right you are," said Delaroche. "I see you know your way about. But I don't quite like that fellow Stubbs stopping behind. He wants to get the start of us, and take all the cream off, confound him! I know his style, but we won't stand his little game." The others seemed to share his ill-humour against Stubbs, and expressed it in vigorous and expressive language, as they generally did when Stubbs was not present.

The day was spent as Hippophil had suggested, in getting provisions from the ship and bringing round the boats.

After a night's rest they began their march into the interior. Hippophil affected to think it unnecessary to take firearms with them, but did not dare to press the matter for fear of exciting suspicion. The fact that they had to carry everything themselves, for they had no horses, disinclined them to take more than a revolver apiece, a few rifles, and a very moderate supply of ammunition. But they took plenty of lassos and bridles.

As they advanced through the lovely country in halcyon weather, over flowery meads, and through fragrant groves of orange and citron trees, and along the banks of babbling streams edged with the oleander, even *their* hardened hearts seemed to feel the sweet influence of nature's entrancing beauty. But what surprised and excited them most was the long, low dwellings of the Houyhnhnms, filled with every

Revolt of the Horses

convenience for the reception of horses, but entirely untenanted by man or beast.

Where were the grooms, who arranged those clean straw litters, and filled the racks with such delicious hay? Where were the horses on whom such loving care was expended? Where, above all, was Stubbs?

Hippophil, of course, was loud in his expressions of surprise and disappointment. The frequent delays, caused by their minute examination of the sheds and their search for Stubbs, prevented their making much progress, and before they had advanced to within two miles of the Houyhnhnm camp evening came on, and they gladly settled themselves in a convenient spot, where they caroused till midnight, and then fell into a drunken sleep. Hippophil alone remained sober and watchful. His first care was to observe the place where the guns were laid, which, with the small store of cartridges, he quietly dropped into a stream which flowed hard by. He then stole quietly into the thicket, and as soon as he thought himself beyond all danger of being seen, he started off towards the Houyhnhnm camp. Having found his patron, Pegasus, he rapidly explained to him the state of affairs, and asked his advice. Hippophil was extremely averse to exposing the lives of the Houyhnhnm to the fire of the marauders, for he was still shuddering at the fearful tragedy he had lately witnessed. After a short deliberation it was resolved to send a body of Yahoos, under the direction of a working horse, to surprise and destroy the gang in their sleep; while the Houyhnhnms were to advance at a short distance in the rear, attended by Hippophil, as a precaution against unforeseen accidents. In about an hour—about two o'clock in the morning—all preparations had been made, and some two hundred of the strongest Yahoos moved stealthily forward in the direction indicated by Hippophil, followed by a squadron of Houyhnhnms. A halt was made at the edge of the thicket which bordered the meadow in which the horse-stealers were lying. Hippophil peered through the bushes, and, to his surprise and terror, saw one of the party rise from his couch and call loudly to Delaroche, who was near him. Not a moment was to be lost. At a word from Hippophil, a working horse gave the signal to the Yahoos, who, with a whoop of delight, rushed forward to the permitted massacre. Meantime, several of the men had risen to their feet, and Delaroche roared out:

"By G——, the monkeys! look out! where are the guns?"

Before the words were well out of his mouth he found himself on the ground in the grasp of a Yahoo, who fixed his teeth in his shoulder, and at the same time clutched his throat with his long finger-nails. Finding his right hand free he contrived with great difficulty to draw his revolver, and discharged it into the belly of his assailant; who let go his hold and rolled over

Revolt of the Horses

with fearful yells. On rising from the ground Delaroche saw that some of his companions had been assailed in nearly the same manner, and he hastened to their assistance. Two or three had been overpowered, and had been torn to pieces or beaten to death with the short sticks which the Yahoos carried. Others had disposed of their adversaries, and standing back to back emptied their revolvers on the surrounding foes, of whom many had fallen, and who now began a retreat into the woods. All at once the firing ceased, and the voice of Walker was now heard above the din, calling out for cartridges. Some of the party rushed to the spot where they had been deposited, and, not finding them, went storming about in all directions with loud cries and execrations. Meanwhile Hippophil had been watching the scene, and saw to his utter dismay that the attack had practically failed, and that the Yahoos were flying in all directions. The critical moment had arrived, and hurrying back to the Houyhnhnms he told them what had happened, and urged them to send forward a hundred of their number in double line to crush the disordered enemy by a rapid charge. This was immediately done, and at a signal from Aethon, who was in the centre of the front line, they dashed across the field with the speed of lightning. Loud cries arose from the terrified marauders—"Cavalry!—Cavalry!"—as they rushed towards the opposite enclosure. But long before they could reach it the Houyhnhnms were upon

Revolt of the Horses

them and over them, and when they wheeled and returned to the charge, not a man was left standing, not a man was left alive; or if any still lingered with shattered limbs they were soon dispatched by the returning Yahoos who, with yells of delight, stripped them of their clothes, for which they wrangled and fought among themselves. An angry neigh from a working Houyhnhnm, however, soon calmed the strife, and they were then employed in bearing off their own dead, and the bodies of the crushed and shattered invaders, and burying them together in a promiscuous heap.

CHAPTER V

ALL was now over. The danger was past; but the effect of recent events on the minds of the Houyhnhnms was deep and lasting. For the first time in the memory of their race the life of one of their number had been cut short by violence. The sight of the bleeding body of their loved sister, outraged and stained by the hand of a loathsome Yahoo, roused hitherto unknown and unimagined sensations in their calm and joyous hearts. They looked with horror on their own feet, defiled by the stain of the foulest blood. It seemed to them that sin had at last entered into their paradise and thrown a dark veil over the fair face of Nature. They had seen bloodshed and death, they had felt wrath and sorrow; they began to tremble for the purity of their own hearts, for the peace of their own souls. Not that they feared death, in the beautiful guise in which it came to them—but such a death!

Although he had taken so prominent a part in the late transactions, and been on the point of losing all that he most prized, Hippophil was probably the least agitated by the recent occurrences. He had lived among *men*, and had seen death in every form—by murder and suicide, in madness and wild debauchery. Like other men,

Revolt of the Horses

he had lived familiarly with every spectacle of horror that the imagination can call up. But to the Houyhnhnms, whose existence was one un-interrupted experience of joy, the murder of the matron was like a moral earthquake, which, for the moment, seemed to shake into ruins the whole fabric of their being.

Slowly and sadly they returned to their accus-tomed haunts and pursuits; even the colts and fillies trotted quietly and demurely beside their dams, as if they, too, felt that some great change had taken place.

As was to be expected, a general assembly was summoned for the following day, for the double purpose of burying the matron and of deliberating on the measures to be adopted in view of the recent events. Hippophil was invited to attend the meeting, which was held in the same place as the one described above. On the right hand of the King, on a kind of stage formed of osier crates, lay the body of Sterope covered with leaves and flowers, towards which all eyes were turned. Behind the King, and somewhat hidden from the assembly, stood Hippophil in a reveren-tial attitude, awaiting the orders of the King, who spoke thus:

"Although by the aid of my own memory and the tradition of my forefathers, my mental vision reaches back to the very origin of our race, I see no such spectacle as that which meets our eyes to-day. The sunshine which illumines this land of ours never yet rested on a murdered Houyhnhnm;

Revolt of the Horses

still less on one overmastered by a Yahoo! (A low whinnying murmur ran through the assembly.) I will not dwell on this; the past is irrevocable. We have learned for the first time to know evil in our own persons; let it be ours to make the good prevail. As we have seen, on the one hand, in the miscreants who sought to enslave us, the depths of Yahoo corruption and infamy, we are encouraged, on the other hand, by the perception that even a Yahoo may be influenced by communion with us. Stand forth, Hippophil! and once more receive our thanks." Hippophil timidly advanced and was greeted by loud neighs of welcome and approval. When he had kissed the hoof of the King he resumed his former position. Lampros continued: "I have said, let the past be past, but we know that the future grows out of the past and takes its shape and colour from it. The godlike life we have hitherto led cannot be ours in all its unclouded brightness, in all its intensity of bliss; at all events, not in the immediate future. Our souls are darkened by all that we have heard of the sufferings of our kindred in other lands. We cannot forget that in one country alone there are three millions of Houyhnhnms enslaved to a Yahoo tribe, distinguished from the brutes in our own kennels only by the possession of a glimmering intelligence, which enables them to work the greater mischief to themselves and others. We hear that creatures of our own flesh and blood are imprisoned, mutilated, beaten, wounded, worn down by excessive

Revolt of the Horses

toil in the service of Yahoo cupidity; that different ranks of Houyhnhnms are forced into monstrous connexion—the noble blood and the ivory framework, mingled with the blood and bones of the lower classes, to the detriment of both; that their lives are shortened, and, worse still, their intellect darkened by the most ruthless oppression, as we see in the case of our poor brother here. I learn from Pegasus, who has often conversed with him, that although he is evidently of a very pure, high lineage, he has quite lost many of our highest attributes. He can hardly read our thoughts, and finds great difficulty in communicating with friends in his former home. The operations of Nature, the spiritual life beyond the grave, which are to us as clear as yonder crystal stream, are only dimly visible to him. One characteristic, however, after all, the highest, still remains—incorruptible innocence and virtue. Centuries of oppression, incessant contact with the most vicious and degraded of living beings, have left him free from vice. Like ourselves he is naked and not ashamed; like us he crops the grass of the field and drinks the limpid stream. The comparative deformity of his body, the diseases to which he is subject, are the consequences of a treacherous climate, of close confinement and excessive exertion, and not of inordinate passions or Yahoo-like excesses.

"The knowledge, I say, of all these things has come upon us as a sudden calamity—we cannot divest ourselves of it. Henceforth a heavy re-

Revolt of the Horses

sponsibility will weigh on us. Are we, or are we not, to remain passive—to affect indifference to the cruel fate of our brethren who live towards the setting sun? If we were selfishly to decide to leave them to their fate, to be satisfied with our own halcyon life, *can* we any longer do so? Our land has been invaded; our dear sister done to a foul death by the very same cruel monsters who traffic in the blood and misery of our distant kindred. For the moment we have been saved from further rapine and murder; but *how* saved? By the artifice of a humane Yahoo, rather than by our own strength and wisdom. But may not the attempt be renewed? May not this last remnant of the primeval world, of a race free from sin, free from suffering, living in perfect harmony with Nature and with God, be brought under the dominion of darkness, and sink into the slough of Yahooism?"

The King paused amidst loud manifestations of approval and sympathy. When silence had been restored he made a sign to a Houyhnhnm of great height and magnificent proportions, who stood near the dais, and who then addressed the meeting. His age, which was evidently very great, had in no way affected the grandeur or beauty of his form, and showed itself chiefly in a certain slowness of motion, and the somewhat dimmed lustre of the eyes, from which benevolence still beamed unclouded.

Looking on the King with an expression of affectionate veneration, he said: "My career on

Revolt of the Horses

earth, O King! is nearly ended. In a few years or months I shall be wandering over the everlasting hills, in the eternal light of God's throne, in the company of our beloved, who have gone before me. But my communion with you, and my interest in this dear and happy land will not cease; and before I go, I wish to add my voice to those which have been raised in favour of immediate action for the salvation of our kindred in England—an action in which, alas! I can take no part. Yet we must not conceal from ourselves that this resolution is no trifling one; that the execution of it calls for qualities which have hitherto been latent in us, because there has been no occasion for their exercise. It will require, first of all, self-sacrifice, submission to suffering, humiliation, contact with evil—nay, and this is worse than all, it requires the practice of the art of concealment, hitherto unknown to us. Whoever undertakes this mission to the enslaved Houyhnhnms in the west will have to meet their persecutors with their own weapons—dissimulation and fraud; will have to familiarise himself with deeds of violence and scenes of bloodshed. Are we ready to make this sacrifice? I think we are; but it is a weighty, even a terrible resolution."

These words, uttered slowly and deliberately, but with indescribable dignity, were listened to in respectful silence; and again, as he ceased, loud murmurs of applause arose. Several others addressed the meeting in the same strain, and

Revolt of the Horses

absolute unanimity prevailed. At the suggestion of the last speaker, and with the sanction of the King, it was resolved that a member of the highest class should be sent to England, accompanied by Hippophil; that they should make full reports of the state of things in that country, and, if possible, organise a general revolt of the horses, with a view to their complete emancipation, and the subjugation, or, if necessary, the extermination, of the now dominant tribe of Yahoos. The next question was—Who should go? All were ready, but each one shrank from putting himself forward as the worthiest. After a somewhat lengthened pause, the young Prince Aethon with the white star in his forehead, who stood near his royal father, asked a hearing. Even in that assembly of noble forms, *he* was distinguished by his beauty, strength, and elegance.

His large dark eyes, in which no white was visible, glowed with fire and love; the great veins of his head and neck swelled beneath the satin skin, and the widely dilated nostrils seemed to draw in large draughts of air with a vivid sensation of delight. The King, towards whom he looked, made a sign of assent. " I am young," he said, "and know that many a more experienced Houyhnhnm would gladly undertake this task; but on that very account, because, if I am sacrificed, the loss to the community will not be so great—I say, *send me!*" (Loud applause.) " Be it so," said the King after a slight pause,

73

and with some emotion, " be it so. It is well that one of our royal blood should employ the great gifts of Nature for the good of his race, and justify the privileges he enjoys by the magnitude of the services he renders. And what," he added, "says Hippophil?" Hippophil again came forward and reverentially bowed his assent. He did so with a heavy heart, for he looked forward with unutterable dismay to a return to all the carking cares and miseries of human life. But he had, once for all, determined to do and venture all in the service of his benefactors.

The meeting now resolved itself into a funeral procession. The body of the murdered Houy-hnhnm was borne on a kind of hurdle, resting on the backs of two working horses. The two little children of the deceased walked on each side of the bier. Then followed the King, the royal consort Leucippe, and other members of the royal family; then the noblest in order of seniority, and the rest of the community. After a march of about two miles towards a rocky hill to the east, they halted before a perpendicular wall of rock, in which a tomb had been hewn by the Yahoos, and there they deposited the body, closing the entrance with a large and heavy stone. The whole proceeding—the first of the kind which had ever taken place, for death in its usual friendly guise excited little notice and no regret—was conducted in perfect silence; and at its conclusion each one returned slowly and thoughtfully to his customary occupations.

Frequent consultations now took place between the young Prince, Pegasus, and Hippophil. On one occasion the last expressed a difficulty which had occurred to him as insuperable. He indeed could communicate with the horses of his own country, but how could the Prince make any reports to the King and the Houyhnhnms at home? It was some time before Pegasus understood him; but when he did, he explained, with a look of amusement to the astounded Hippophil, that all the highest class had the power, not only of reading each others' thoughts, but by a peculiar exercise of will (the CRNITGN), of transmitting intelligence at whatever distance to any member of the race. Hippophil listened with awestruck surprise to this new revelation of the divine endowments of these wonderful beings, and thought, with a melancholy smile, of the electric telegraph, the telephone, the "thought-reading," and the spiritualism of his own poor feeble and benighted fellow-men. Could these things be really a faint reminiscence of some glorious faculty possessed in the days of purity, and now lost? Was the recovery of these powers still possible?

He was roused from the waking dream into which he had fallen by Pegasus, who suggested to him a real difficulty, asking him how he proposed to convey the Prince and himself to England? Staggered by this direct question, to

Revolt of the Horses

which he could at first find no answer, he suddenly
remembered the boats and the ship from which
the marauders had landed. Begging permission
to absent himself for a time he hastened to the
cliffs, from which he saw the boats high and
dry above the tide mark, and the vessel still
riding peacefully in the offing. Returning to
Pegasus he made him acquainted with these
facts and of his intention to go on board the
ship and secure a passage. On the following
morning, therefore, he launched the smallest
of the three boats, with the help of a few
Yahoos under the command of a working horse;
and, as the wind was blowing gently from the
shore, he had no difficulty in reaching the ship.
Long before he arrived he was seen by those on
board, who for some days had been looking for
the return of their shipmates. He was therefore
received with eager welcome and curiosity by
the remnant of the crew, consisting of the
captain, the boatswain, and ten sailors. Great
was the astonishment of all on beholding Hippophil, who was supposed to have been lost on
the *Mongolia*. The first question was whether
he had seen Stubbs, Walker, and Delaroche, and
what was the cause of their delay; and then—
Had they found the horses they told such lies
about? Hippophil, who had carefully prepared
his tale, made the following report. He himself had been cast on shore in a state of insensibility, together with his thoroughbred horse. On
coming to his senses he found himself surrounded

Revolt of the Horses

by a kind of white baboons, exactly like men in form, who, without hurting him, carried them both to a shed where they found oats and hay, on which, with fruit, they had subsisted for several weeks. One day he descried a boat in the distance, and to his great joy soon saw his friends Stubbs, Walker, and Delaroche land on the island. They explained to him the object of their visit, and he undertook to show them a herd of wild horses, which he had seen a few miles in the interior of the country. After considerable trouble they had managed to secure a magnificent young colt with the lasso. A dispute then arose between Stubbs, who assumed a very imperious tone, on the one side, and Delaroche and Walker on the other, concerning the possession of the horse, and a free fight began between them and their respective backers. Having no interest in the strife, he said, he had hidden himself in a cave hard by. When the firing ceased he had come out and, to his horror, found the whole party stretched on the ground, either dying or badly wounded. He had afforded what little assistance he could to those who were still alive; and while busily employed in this way he saw, just before nightfall, a horde of the white monkeys, who, advancing on all fours, rushed with horrible yells upon the scene. He had scarcely time to escape to his cave when the beasts were upon them. His ears were pierced by the screams of the wounded men, but in a few minutes all was still, and when he ventured forth again, the white monkeys had disappeared, and he found nothing but the mangled bodies of his friends, who had been stripped of their clothes. Seeing that they were past all help, and in mortal fear lest the monkeys should return, he had made off to the coast, and managed to reach the boats without being seen.

His recital was received by the diminished crew with great surprise, and, it must be confessed, with little real sorrow. If any regret was felt for the absence of their mates, it arose from a doubt whether they would be able to work the ship without them. Another cause of anxiety, however, soon presented itself: How should they clear themselves from the suspicion of the authorities of Cape Town, when they returned with only about a third of their number? How would Hippophil's account be received? At all events it was absolutely necessary that he should return with them to give his evidence. They therefore eagerly offered him a free passage and maintenance for himself and horse, if he could bring him off; and they besought him to return to the island with two or three men and bring away the boats. Hippophil, of course, gladly closed with this offer, and strongly advised that those who went with him should remain in the boats at a short distance from land, until he was able to rejoin them under favour of night. To this they agreed the more readily, as they were terrified at the thought of falling into the hands of the white apes, and

Revolt of the Horses

not at all inclined to renew the attempt on the horses, in which their comrades had so miserably failed.

At nightfall Hippophil returned to the island with four men, leaving only six on board, including the captain, who saw them depart with great anxiety. On reaching the shore they launched the larger boats with considerable difficulty, and anchored them a little way out. Hippophil made his way back to his usual quarters, and after a sleepless night sought out Pegasus, to whom he reported the success of his mission. Pegasus communicated this to the King, and an assembly was called for noon of the same day. In private conversation with the Prince, Hippophil respectfully begged him to consider the tremendous nature of the task he was undertaking and the uncertainty of success. He set before him the dangers of the voyage, the hardships and the difficulties he would meet with, and above all the humiliation—so intolerable to one of his noble nature and intellectual superiority — which he would have to undergo. "If our mission is to succeed" said Hippophil, with tears in his eyes, "I, too, shall have to treat you as if you were my property, my beast of burden. You will have to bear my continual presence, and that of others worse than myself. How can you forgive me if I use you as men use their horses?—if I mount your back?—control your free actions with bit and bridle?" The loose and glossy skin of the young Houyhnhnm

79

Revolt of the Horses

quivered as he listened; his glorious eyes dilated, and with a loud snort of disgust he leapt into the air. But he soon calmed himself, and turning towards Hippophil, who had fallen on his knees, he bade him rise, saying, " I will bear all things at your hands, knowing that what you do is done with a worthy object."

Then followed the assembly, which was attended by vast numbers of Houyhnhnms, some of them from a great distance. It had become widely known that Aethon was about to depart, and everyone was anxious to see him, perhaps for the last time. His mother, a queenly matron of matchless beauty, reclined on the dais, and regarded her noble offspring with affection and pride, and something like pity in her soft eyes, but she forbore all complaint. What he was doing was worthy of himself and his race, and she would not if she could divert him from his purpose. Only, as they left the meeting, she passed her beautiful neck over his head, and then gently raised her ebony hoof to his breast, as if in the act of blessing him. The King, too, rested his upraised nose on the crest of his son, and the whole assembly looked on with sympathy and loyal affection at these unwonted marks of deep, yet restrained emotion. Aethon, too, though visibly touched, bore himself with spirit and dignity. Hippophil alone shed bitter tears at the thought of what they had to undergo, and at his own exclusion from the paradise of beauty and love in which he had been so blessed. He

Revolt of the Horses

parted with the greatest regret from his faithful friend Bend'or, who, by the permission of the King, was left on the island.

According to the wish of Hippophil, the Prince and he were allowed to go down to the shore alone, that the men in the boat might not see the other Houyhnhnms. The embarkation was somewhat difficult, but as Aethon made no resistance, and quickly understood what was required of him, it was at last effected, and both arrived safely at the ship's side. Use was made of the hoisters which had been carefully prepared by Stubbs and Delaroche for their expected stud of horses, and Aethon was soon safely lodged in a horse-box on deck, which Hippophil made as comfortable as circumstances would allow.

CHAPTER VI

THE voyage to the Cape was, on the whole, prosperous ; but for a few hours a brisk gale prevailed, and Aethon became acquainted with what we call "weather"—a new idea to a Houyhnhnm —and experienced sea-sickness, which is even worse to a horse than to a man, because the former cannot relieve himself. As they drew near to Cape Town on the tenth day, Hippophil was careful to cover his charge as much as possible with clothes, to conceal his magnificent proportions from the eyes of the public. The landing was effected without much difficulty in the early morning, and Hippophil was fortunate in finding a loose-box in a roomy and airy stable, in which Aethon was lodged by himself—without, of course, being confined by halters or partitions. Hippophil heard, with great relief, that Lord Salford — a meeting with whom he especially dreaded—was confined to his bed by the effects of a long series of convivial meetings, which had affected his brain, and rendered all communication with him impossible. As soon as the affair of the missing crew and passengers (who were deeply regretted by the numerous persons to whom they owed money) had been settled, and the survivors exonerated by the testimony of Hippophil, the latter

Revolt of the Horses

began to make his preparations for the voyage to England. He made the acquaintance of Captain Fellows of the fine ship *Africa*, just about to start for Southampton, and found him ready to provide the Prince with exceptionally comfortable quarters.

Aethon seemed interested and amused by the strange novelty of his surroundings; but he evidently suffered much from the climate, and the presence of the human Yahoos who surrounded him. His keen intelligence soon penetrated through the surface to the essence of the new phenomena, and his mind was fully occupied in the study of the great mass of humanity of which he had hitherto seen only a single representative, and that one largely modified by Houyhnhnm influences. The impression made on him was not favourable, as he listened day after day to the conversation of those who gathered near his stall, which, by an exercise of his will, he was soon able to understand. During the passage he became better and better acquainted with the extraordinary skill with which men bend the forces of nature to their wishes and aims, and more and more astonished and disgusted at the utter futility of those wishes, the selfish meanness of those aims. Accustomed as he was to enjoy the highest pleasures of the intellect and the senses, the rapture of inspiration both poetic and religious, he observed with pitying amazement the painful efforts with which these poor creatures strove to squeeze one drop of pleasure, one *soupçon* of flavour, from the Dead Sea apples in the attainment of which they spent their lives. A flood of

Revolt of the Horses

new sensation and new knowledge poured in upon his heart and mind ; but it was the knowledge of evil which shocked and saddened him. Now arose in him the sense of martyrdom in a holy cause, which he had voluntarily offered to undergo, but of which he had hardly realised the intense un-utterable bitterness. Nor were his physical suffer-ings inconsiderable. Hippophil, indeed, did what he could to mitigate these, by the most assiduous and respectful care ; but he saw with pain the sensitive nerves of the noble creature, which had hitherto only vibrated with pleasure to the influences of external Nature, now quivering with pain in the damp air, and under the sting of the raw and biting breezes. The narrow confinement, too, of the horse-box was a kind of torture to one who had been accustomed to range at will over the broad plains, and beneath the scented shades of the wide forests of his island home.

Among the passengers was the Earl of Pevensey, an English nobleman of great abilities and high distinction, who, in his youth, before the abolition of the House of Peers, had been a prominent Member of Parliament. He was now on his return from a tour round the world, the chief object of which was to see the distant lands which had once been under the dominion of England. He wished to see, with his own eyes, the present state of that Greater Britain which he had once helped to rule. His interest in horses—for, like so many great statesmen of former generations, he was an ardent fox-hunter and a patron of the turf—soon led him to the horse-box of the Prince, where he got into conversation with Hippophil, whose singular character strongly attracted him. Very frequent, therefore, were his visits to the Prince, whose magnificent form, though concealed as much as possible by clothes, struck him with the greatest admiration. When the weather was tolerably fine he was accompanied by his daughter, Lady Ermyntrude Milbourne, a girl between seventeen and eighteen years old, the darling of her widowed father. It would be impossible to do justice to the charms of this sweet, just opening, human flower. Suffice it to say that she was slightly above the middle height, of an exquisitely-moulded form, "whose gestures beamed with mind," and that she had an abundance of fair hair, a complexion of milk and roses, and large blue eyes "of heaven's own tint," full of intelligence and innocent tender-ness. Hippophil was charmed by her enthusiastic expressions of delight on first seeing Aethon's head and face, and while he jealously, and even fiercely, guarded his charge from the notice of the other passengers, he was so far won upon by the gentle sweetness of Lady Ermyntrude as to make an exception in her favour. As he looked on her he forgot his disgust for his own race, and the words of the old poet sounded in his ears:

> "Her lips are like the budded roses
> Whom ranks of lilies neighbour nigh;
> Within whose bounds she balm encloses,
> Apt to entice a Deity."

The Prince himself, who had started back with

Revolt of the Horses

dilated nostrils and a shudder of disgust when she first laid her little hand on the shining white star of his broad forehead, was soon reconciled to her presence, and was interested in the phenomenon of a perfectly pure-minded, noble, and unselfish creature—for he read her every thought—in the form of a female Yahoo! Towards the father, Lord Pevensey, he never unbent, and it was a matter of roguish delight and pride to Ermyntrude that she alone, besides Hippophil, was allowed to caress the noble creature, to fondle his beautiful nose, and to reach him bread or fruit.

"Not a bad judge that horse of yours," said Lord Pevensey to Hippophil, laughing, as he saw his daughter kiss the white star on Aethon's forehead. "When *I* go near him he snorts at me as if I were a camel or a traction engine. It would take a good man to ride him. What do you mean to do with him? You had better sell him to Lady Ermyntrude." Hippophil answered evasively, for in fact he had not made up his mind on the subject, though it was seldom absent from his thoughts.

The Prince, as we have said, was greatly puzzled by Ermyntrude, and often questioned Hippophil about her. Was she really of the same blood as the other Yahoos — really the daughter of that man? Was there ever one like her? How could she associate with the rest of her species, whose persons, sentiments, and character could only repel and disgust her?

Hippophil smiled and sighed at the same time.

Revolt of the Horses

"There are not many," he said, "who combine in such a very high degree physical and moral excellence, but they *are* met with, especially in this sex and age. She has been reared in exceptionally favourable circumstances. She has lived in houses filled with works of the noblest art, in beautiful parks and gardens, and lovely scenery, in which Nature has been allowed to take its own sweet way. Her mind has been carefully developed, and directed towards the noblest objects. She has been surrounded by an atmosphere of affection, and her naturally pure and lofty aspirations were wisely and tenderly fostered by a saintly mother, raised above the mists of error and passion, and taught to expand in the purer and brighter regions of the Christian's heaven. The rapture of emotion —the full abiding sense of the Divine presence and favour—which are universal among you— sometimes fall for a brief period to the lot of these, and they stand, as it were, transfigured before God." "And what is the end?" said the Prince. "Do they live in perpetual isolation from the vile creatures of the outer world? How else can they remain what they are?" Hippophil was silent for a few moments, and then replied slowly and sadly, "They seldom remain what they are. They go out into 'the world,' and generally, sooner or later, succumb to its evil influences. Women have a deplorable facility in sinking to the level of their surroundings, and change colour like the chameleon in different atmospheres."

Revolt of the Horses

Hippophil was unwilling to pursue the subject. The renewed contact with his fellow-men filled him with sad thoughts, and the weight of human crime and human misery once more weighed heavily upon his soul. He, therefore, turned his attention to the practical question of their *modus operandi* in England. Would it be better to form some connection with a powerful patron like Lord Pevensey and enter his service? An opportunity would be thereby afforded of coming into contact with the noblest breed of horses in England, and of instructing them in the object of the Prince's mission. The latter saw at once the advantages of such a course, and Hippophil took an early opportunity of broaching the subject to Lord Pevensey. He could not for a moment think of selling Aethon, or giving any one the right to control his movements. His proposal was, to retain the full ownership of the Prince, but to place him in his lordship's training stables, and, if it was thought desirable, to allow him to run in some great race with Lord Pevensey's colours. His chief stipulations were that Aethon should be lodged in a separate building, and that no one should be allowed access to him without his permission. Lord Pevensey was somewhat surprised at these singular conditions, and before coming to a final understanding desired to examine the Prince's points more closely. To this Hippophil could not but assent; and going to Aethon he warned him of the coming ordeal, and begged him to restrain his indignation at

Revolt of the Horses

being inspected and handled by a Yahoo. An opportunity was taken at a very early hour, when no other passengers were on deck, to submit the Prince to Lord Pevensey's judgment. Lady Ermyntrude was also present when the clothing was taken off him and he stepped out of the horse-box. Lord Pevensey was an excellent judge of a horse, and was at first struck dumb with amazement as his eye wandered over Aethon's broad chest, the elegant slope of his muscular shoulders, the charmingly tapering head, with a muzzle over which a lady's armlet might be passed, his flat and exquisitely-turned legs. But as he continued his delighted scrutiny, and examined point after point of the harmonious form, he broke forth into the most enthusiastic expressions of delight. "Never in his wildest dreams had he imagined such a horse! Where was he bred? Who were his sire and dam? How could such blood be unknown to the stud-book? What a miserable set of seedy hacks would his own admired stud—one of the finest in England —appear by the side of this marvel of Nature and training!" Lady Ermyntrude, too, was beside herself with delight, and lavished every term of endearment and every fond caress on the noble animal. Aethon, though inwardly chafing at the humiliation he was undergoing, remained quite passive, until Lord Pevensey proceeded to force open his mouth. Then his patience forsook him, and with a shiver of disgust he threw up his head, while his eyes flashed with indignation.

Revolt of the Horses

"Hallo!" said Lord Pevensey, "how about temper, Mr Hippophil? or is he ashamed of his age?" "Let me try," said Ermyntrude; and first stroking his nose, she gently drew his jaws asunder so as to give a good view of his teeth. "Not three years old! By jove, what a colt! what a colt!" cried the Earl; "but how in the world have you managed to get round the high and mighty beast, Ermy? I expect you'll have to turn breaker of unmanageable horses." He now readily assented to Hippophil's conditions, declaring that merely to look at such an animal was a liberal education; and his daughter was enchanted to hear that her glorious pet was to be taken to their own home in Sussex.

The rest of the voyage, which lasted about three weeks, was uneventful, though in stormy weather — very trying to Aethon — and they arrived safely at Southampton in January. Lord Pevensey with his daughter and their attendants were conveyed by train to Longwood. Hippophil travelled with the Prince in a horse-box. The earl offered the hospitality of his house to Hippophil, for whom he had conceived a sincere regard, but the latter naturally preferred the company of Aethon, and was, moreover, too anxious about his safety to let him out of sight. The unused stable of a dower-house on the edge of the park was assigned to him, and Hippophil nominally occupied the upper rooms; but the greater part of his time was spent in the society and the service of the Prince.

Revolt of the Horses

Although the contrast between the paradise he had left and the place of his exile was infinitely great, the Prince could hardly have been better situated than he was. The noble park, with its magnificent trees and grassy slopes, bore some resemblance, even in winter, which was happily a mild one, to the forest glades in which he had been reared. His least unpleasant hours were those in which he was left to range alone through the avenues, or along the banks of the clear river, which flowed at the bottom of the gentle hill on which the mansion stood.

Yet, even in this peaceful solitude, he could not escape from sights and sounds which told him of the never-ending martyrdom of his race. On one occasion he was moving rapidly along the boundary of the park, close to a road, on the other side of which a cottage was being built. As he looked through the bushes down upon a narrow lane below, he saw a poor lean old horse vainly endeavouring to drag a heavy cartload of bricks up the hill. The task was utterly beyond his power; yet the brute who was driving him urged him on by oaths and savage cuts from a cruel whip. After a last frantic effort, he fell prostrate on the ground, with the shaft of the cart pressing heavily on his leg. The blows and curses were now redoubled on the fainting animal, but his senses were beyond the reach of suffering, and his eyes already swam in death. Aethon, excited beyond all control by this terrible spectacle, sprang over the hedge at a bound, and launching his hind legs at the head of the man, laid him prostrate and senseless on the body of the dying horse. He addressed the latter with sympathising words, but the spirit had already fled to the happy pastures of departed Houyhnhnms.

Full of the most painful thoughts, and with a sense of contamination accruing from the violent act of retributive justice he had exercised, Aethon returned to his abode, steeled in his purpose to bear, and to dare *anything* in the cause of his oppressed brethren, and for the extermination of their cruel oppressors. He heard afterwards that the carter had been found dead in the lane, but that the cause of his death was unknown.

The deliberations of Aethon and Hippophil were often, and not unpleasantly, interrupted by visits from Lady Ermyntrude, who thought the day ill passed in which she did not see her favourite, and bring some dainty for his consumption. She was always making some arrangement for his comfort and pleasure, and suggested, among other things, that it might enliven the dreariness of the stable if a window were opened in the wall towards the road, so that he could see all that passed by without being seen himself. She also got her father to improve the warming apparatus, that the young Houyhnhnm might suffer less from changes in the temperature.

From this window Aethon watched with keen interest the thoroughbred horses, belonging to Lord Pevensey, which were every morning led or ridden to the exercising ground by their

Revolt of the Horses

respective grooms. The latter were very curious to learn something of what they called the "dark" horse, on whom such extraordinary care was lavished, and they often pulled up their horses in front of his stable. He recognised at once that these future race-horses were originally descended from the purest Houyhnhnm blood, and observed with satisfaction and pride, that hundreds of years of slavery had failed to obliterate the traces of their lofty lineage. Even now, as compared with their Yahoo owners and attendants, they looked like gods in exile. One morning, as they halted before his open window, he addressed them in the purest Houyhnhnm dialect. The effect on the thoroughbreds was like that of an electric shock, and they one and all began neighing, rearing, dancing, and curvetting, in a manner very embarrassing to their riders. The high commanding tone in which Aethon spoke, and the strangeness of his accent, struck them with the utmost astonishment, and they listened to the sound as if it had been a voice from heaven. When "*order* was restored," the Prince, in a few short sentences, told them his own history, revealed to them their kinship with the race from which he sprang, and explained to them the objects of his mission. He could say no more on this occasion, but he found opportunities, in the course of their frequent visits, of questioning them as to their present state, the manner in which they passed their lives, and the treatment they received at the hands of the Yahoos. He then tried to find out whether they were still capable of receiving intelligence from him without the intervention of speech, and at *any* distance, and was delighted to learn that this glorious faculty, the CRNITGN, though weakened, was not extinct, and would soon be completely restored by exercise. After a short time, he found it no longer essential to see or speak to them, but he continually flooded their minds and hearts with valuable information and noble sentiments. From nearly all he met with a hearty response. They gladly undertook to exercise themselves in what we may call mental telephony, which would enable them to communicate with their brethren in other parts of the kingdom, and to secure their allegiance to their heaven-born, heaven-sent leader.

Although, of course, there was no danger of discovery or betrayal of the projected rising against their tyrants, those who had the charge of horses did not fail to observe an extraordinary ferment among them. From all quarters came frequent accounts of accidents arising from the restiveness and sudden violence of horses; and some observant persons began to speak of a prevalent mania, akin to "staggers." The general insubordination was met, of course, by increased severity and restraint, which, again, only intensified the excitement of the maltreated animals, and their longing to be released from their galling chains.

CHAPTER VII

FROM time to time Aethon communicated his observations on what he saw around him to his royal sire, by whom they were made known to the rest of the community. The most interesting of these reports concerned the position of their kindred in England.

"There are," said the Prince, "no less than three million so-called 'horses' in this country, divided into classes or 'breeds'—*i.e.* artificial developments of the original type—created and modified to suit the various offices they are destined to perform—no regard whatever being had to the inclination or interests of individuals. These 'breeds' by no means correspond with the natural and ineffaceable distinctions between the three orders of Houyhnhmns—the royal, the noble, and the working classes—based on essential differences in their physical and mental powers. The highest breed, as being the swiftest, are set apart in their youth for competitive trials of speed, and are treated, comparatively speaking, with indulgence. They are surrounded with every comfort compatible with slavery, and are carefully served by a certain class of Yahoos, who make a study of their qualities, and of the treatment most conducive to their preservation and development.

95

Revolt of the Horses

Yet even these are forced in extreme youth to exhaust their strength and destroy their constitutions by premature and excessive exertion in the racecourse, and are ruthlessly sacrificed to the vanity and greed of their owners. When their prime is past they are cast out of their comfortable quarters, and degraded to the meanest uses under the lowest class of Yahoos. The other 'breeds' arise from an indiscriminate 'crossing' of horses of every class; and while some are to be seen of a size and strength approaching the working members of our community, there are others no bigger than a donkey. The reckless disregard of the nature and feelings of our miserable kinsmen is incorporated and manifested in the person of a creature called a mule—the offspring of an ass and a horse, a monster which, happily, Nature repudiates, and denies the power of reproduction. I often wonder whether the perception of these human Yahoos is really so blunt that they have no inkling of the true nature of the creatures whom they maltreat and abuse — whether they can really have lived side by side with them for thousands of years without ever discovering their true place in creation, their vast superiority to themselves. In this connection, I learn from Hippophil the curious fact that the possession of horses has in all ages been a source of honour to the highest class of Yahoos, and that, among nations widely differing from one another, titles of nobility have been derived from words signifying horse or rider—as Eques, Chevalier, Ritter, etc.

Revolt of the Horses

In ancient Greece, he says, from which *all* the
little wisdom possessed by the Yahoos comes,
they must have had some idea of the original
nobility of the horse, since, on the face of the
noblest temple in Athens, there were marble
images of them which might almost vie in majesty
and beauty with the form of a Houyhnhnm.
Hippophil further informs me that the greatest
of Greek poets, when he wishes to do honour to
a country or a people, calls the former 'horse-
breeding,' and the latter 'horse-taming.' Their
greatest conqueror too, built a sepulchre and a
tower over the remains of his charger Bucephalus.
The Roman Emperors, who managed to bring all
the tribes of Yahoos under their sway, and beat
the vile creatures into something like obedience
and order, showed the greatest honour to the
horse. One of them made his horse consul (or
governor) at Rome, an act at which these purblind Yahoos pretend to laugh; others set up
golden and marble statues of horses in their
temples. Something like remorse, too, seems
occasionally to have touched the callous hearts of
more modern Yahoos, for Hippophil has repeated
to me some lines, by an Italian, in which he
describes the death of the famous charger of
Orlando, called 'Vegliantin,' at the battle of
Roncevalles, and makes the Yahoo knight say:

> O Vegliantin s'io ti feci mai torto!
> Perdonami, ti priego, cosi morto!

"Even now, and here, the entire fabric of what
they call civilisation—of which more hereafter—

rests entirely on the labour of horses. These are the companions of the working Yahoos, and bear with them the burden and heat of the day. They help them to force from an unwilling soil and a miserable climate the means of bare existence for the many, and of baleful luxury for the few. They transport from place to place the thousand objects with which men try to maintain or adorn their miserable lives; they enable these restless and dissatisfied creatures, who are incapacitated by hereditary weakness from using their own limbs, to move rapidly over the face of the earth. In almost every department of human life the co-operation of the horse is absolutely indispensable, and it is on this fact that my hopes of emancipating our suffering brethren are mainly founded."

Hippophil meantime was looking forward with anxiety to the time when, according to his promise, the Prince was to be put into training for the Derby. He knew, of course, that the immeasurable superiority of the young Houyhnhnm rendered all preparation, except that of learning to tolerate a weight on his back, superfluous and absurd. But he could not venture to reveal either his antecedents or his true nature; and if he had done so he would only have been regarded as a lunatic. But how could he bear to see the glorious being whom he served, bridled and saddled and mounted by a trainer or a jockey? How could Aethon, in spite of his high resolve, endure it? But there was no escape, and

Revolt of the Horses

Hippophil was obliged to forewarn him that on the following day Lord Pevensey would come with his trainer and a famous jockey, to make trial of his paces and his temper in the park. He proposed to save him from the first contact with these people by being the first to mount him, earnestly beseeching him, at the same time, not to resent the indignity to which he was compelled to subject him.

At the appointed time the earl appeared with his trainer, Mr Horrock, and a famous jockey, called "Baby Ned," from Newmarket. The outward appearance of the last named eminent personage, to whom many of the noblest and wealthiest men in England, and "of honourable women not a few," paid court, was not calculated to lessen the disgust of the Prince at the idea of submitting to his control. The name of "Baby" was very appropriate to his small round figure and chubby cheeks; he might even have been called "infant," for his head was as totally devoid of hair as that of a new-born child; but he covered the defect by a well-oiled wig. Though he had neither the stature nor the face of a man, it was evident from his swollen eyes and pimply face, and the expression of cunning about his mouth, that he had had time to acquire most of the vices of manhood, and that he "knew his way about," as he boasted. His skill as a horseman was beyond all question, and brought him in a very large income. Standing with his short legs wide apart, and with a cigar half his own length in his mouth,

Revolt of the Horses

he surveyed the magnificent proportions of Aethon with half-closed eyes, and condescended to express his approval in his own vile turf-jargon. Half displeased at being unable to find any faults in Aethon himself, he made up for it by expressing great dissatisfaction at not being able to get any information respecting his antecedents.

Who was his sire? What mare was he out of? How the blast! was he to ride a horse without being able to give his pedigree? Why, he should get laughed at all over England. However, he didn't mind throwing a leg over him and giving him a canter to try his pace and form, but he would not promise to ride him at Epsom—for who could trust a horse when you didn't know the strain, etc.?

The poor Prince eyed the miserable little creature—in whom all the basest qualities of the Yahoo seemed intensified—with unutterable contempt, wondering that the earth should breed such vermin. Lord Pevensey and his daughter were present, and the latter, patting the proud neck of her favourite, besought Ned to be very gentle with him, and above all not to use his spurs, which she said were *quite* unnecessary. The Baby smiled superior, murmuring to himself that "muslin was no good in a racing-stable," and climbed into the saddle. Hippophil shuddered at the sight, and pretending to make some alteration in the bridle, he begged the Prince in a low tone to be patient. Away they sped along a measured mile in the park. Lord Pevensey and the trainer timed them,

Revolt of the Horses

watch in hand, and found to their utter amazement that the distance had been covered in fifty seconds, and that without apparent distress.

The Baby thought that they had made a mistake, "For," said he, "he didn't spread himself at all. We can beat that. Mind and be accurate this time."

Starting off again, he began to use whip and spur, and the lookers on saw Aethon suddenly stop in full career. The prick of the spur in his side acted on him like a violent electric shock, and he stopped dead short in utter bewilderment. Ned, who was nearly unseated by the suddenness of the change, flew into a rage, and, with a flood of oaths, dug his spurs once more into the Prince's side. The contest between man and "horse" was of short duration. In a few seconds the Baby was sent flying into the air like a tennis-ball from a bat, and was taken up bleeding and insensible. Aethon, though quivering with excitement and pain, walked slowly back to Hippophil, who led him to his loose-box, and as soon as possible relieved him of saddle and bridle, the signs of servitude, and washed his lacerated sides. Some of Ned's friends seemed inclined to inflict punishment on the Prince, but Lord Pevensey would not allow this, saying that it was Ned's fault in using his spurs. The latter, who escaped with a broken rib, was furious at having been unseated, and declared that he would pay the brute off some day; that he was an ill-bred devil, as might be expected from a beast which had no pedigree to show. The earl was greatly disappointed at the result of the trial, and expressed his fears to Hippophil that all hope of winning the Derby with Aethon was at an end. Lady Ermyntrude was secretly on the Prince's side, and though she could not but feel some pity for the Baby's disaster, she thought no worse of her favourite.

" I wish I might ride you," she said, patting his satin neck. " I know you would not hurt me, you dear old boy."

So saying, she left the stables with her father, leaving Aethon in a state of astonishment at himself, at being able to bear the presence of a Yahoo without repugnance, and even with some degree of pleasure. As Ned was looked on as the first flat-race rider in England, and his report of the Prince was likely to be accepted in every racing and sporting centre, Lord Pevensey gave up all thought of entering him for the Derby in his own name, but readily allowed Hippophil to do so, and to occupy the dower-house stables as long as he pleased.

The late events only increased the Prince's ardour in carrying on the work of preparing the minds of the horses in England for the great revolt. He also continued to communicate the results of his observations and the information he gained from conversation with Hippophil to his friends at home.

" The more," he said, " I see and hear of the inhabitants of this land, the more perplexed I am. They seem to be akin to our Yahoos, for they are identical in form, and have all their

Revolt of the Horses

vile appetites and passions in an exaggerated degree. Yet there is an extraordinary difference between the two tribes, which implies either a different origin, or what is more probable, the utter extinction in our own Yahoos of the faculty of reason. According to tradition, men were once pure and noble, full of love to one another, and friends of God. From this state they fell, but unlike our Yahoos, they have not lost the remembrance of that former state; and have not, or had not, some nineteen hundred years ago, entirely forfeited the favour of their Creator. When at an earlier period He thought fit to destroy the whole human race as being too vile to live, He preserved one family alive, which, as was hoped, would re-people the world with a new and better generation. This hope, too, proved futile, for the latent germ of sin spread once more through the hearts and minds of the few survivors, and poisoned the sources of their life. Again and again the Almighty hand was held out from heaven to the fallen world, until, about nineteen hundred years ago, a divine Being, a Person of the Triune God, came down from heaven to drive sin from the earth, and to restore mankind to its pristine nobility and purity. For a time the heavenly mission seemed to be successful. The divine light was shed abroad, the divine presence was once more felt, and heaven was opened to the aspirations and the view of all who purified themselves from evil. There can be no doubt that multitudes began to taste the joy which fills our hearts, and to commune in spirit even here with the souls of those who had gone before them. The teaching and commands of the divine Saviour were recorded, and a powerful institution called the Church was formed, to be an ark and refuge of the soul from the foul waters of corruption. But the prospect was soon clouded. The fabric of the Church was built of incongruous materials, and the old Yahoo pride and passion, greed and lust, soon spread themselves through all its members. The dark pall was once more drawn between heaven and earth, and the divine voices were no longer heard or heeded.

"Yet indications were never wanting that the remembrance of that better state, that capacity for a diviner life, were not entirely lost. Through some small crevice an occasional ray of heavenly light illumined here and there some human soul. They have traditions of Saints who held direct communion with God, who enjoyed for brief periods the ecstatic rapture which is our normal life, and in whose hearts glowed the universal love which is our common heritage. But these cases, always rare, have become rarer and rarer. Even now the Church exists in name, and the principles of the divine Saviour are professed and taught. Thousands of these Yahoos, who hate and injure and oppress one another, who prefer the lowest sensual pleasure to communion with the divine spirit, will assemble together to hear such precepts as these: 'Love thy neigh-

Revolt of the Horses

bour as thyself'—'Flee lusts'—'Live in charity
with all men'—'Love God.' They even pro-
fess complete faith in the excellence of these
precepts, but they seldom allow them to influence
their conduct or their actions. Selfishness reigns
supreme. The great object, the chief delight of
every human Yahoo, is to secure some advantage
exclusively for *himself;* and all objects lose their
lustre in his eyes directly they are shared by
others. But though sin and selfishness are
almost universal, there are still great differences
between man and man in intellectual powers.
It would seem as if there had once existed
different orders among them as among us, endowed with different faculties. A few seem to
have faint glimmerings of the higher powers,
while most of them are mere machines, moved
by selfish instincts and passions, without con-
science, pity, or remorse. The appearance from
time to time of men whom they call poets and
saints seems to indicate this original distinction
of orders. But these intellectual and moral
heights are now seldom witnessed, and are
gradually sinking to the level of the putrid
swamps of common humanity.

" The chief agents in obliterating the distinctions
of type and rank, which probably once existed
among them, are their astounding social arrangements and relations, founded on the universal
passion which they call love—thus degrading
what should be an entirely noble word. This
inordinate feeling of desire entertained by one

sex for the other seizes on nearly all, and unites in foul bonds the comparatively noble with the utterly base. There is little or no rational selection in their marriages. The consequence is that the basest Yahoo blood, with all the vile passions which circulate in it, taints the entire race, and there is no longer any real distinction of classes. If the lowest and basest male Yahoo, devoid of physical beauty, intellect, or morals, becomes possessed of an accumulated store of food, or luxuries, or toys, he is able to command the services of those of higher organisation, and may mingle his base nature with that of the most refined and gifted females of the land. The appalling evils arising from the passion of 'love' are so evident, that even the Yahoos make some weak attempts to restrain and regulate it. What they call morality — *i.e.* a certain moderation in the indulgence of the passions—is inculcated on the mass of the people ; but the law is invariably relaxed in favour of the powerful and the rich. Any great distinction, whether it be extraordinary personal beauty, enormous wealth, high rank, eminence as a popular speaker, writer, or actor, exempts the possessor of it from all moral laws. Those, for example, who denounce the sin of incontinence or adultery when the delinquent is weak or poor, will pay honour to the privileged sinner, and unite themselves to him by the closest ties. In our eyes there is scarcely any appreciable difference between one Yahoo and another in respect of beauty—they are all alike, hideous. But among these human Yahoos, the greatest possible importance is attached to slight differences of form, feature, and colour, which are hardly perceptible to us. Hence it comes that, while one female Yahoo is the object of the admiration and mad passion of thousands of males, others are utterly contemned and neglected. But they are all well aware of the general deformity of their own persons, the sight of which is only tolerable even to themselves in the short period of youth. They, therefore, seek to hide it from one another by the use of dress, such as you saw on Hippophil. Were they to appear as their first parents are said to have done, and as we, of course, still do, in a state of nudity, the sight would be too shocking even for their gross eyes. They therefore endeavour to attract the attention of their fellow-Yahoos by the use of garments of various shapes and colours, and to make themselves forget the hideous form which they conceal. For the better attainment of this object of concealment, they are extremely careful that these garments shall not betray the lines and proportions of the figure ; this is especially the case among the females. Sometimes their dress stands out on all sides in a circular form, so as entirely to hide the lower limbs. At other times they wear a sort of hump on the lower part of the back, and pile up their hair on the top of the head. In this country, but not, I hear, in all, the face is left uncovered, filling the beholder

Revolt of the Horses

with immense disgust; but they carefully cover the feet, and sometimes the hands, with the skin of some dead animal.

"They differ from our Yahoos in this respect, that, although their mental capacity does not enable them to comprehend truth in its entirety, they are continually striving to attain it, and making all kinds of discordant and contradictory guesses respecting what is good and true. What is to *us* clear and certain is matter of conjecture, doubt, and dispute to *them*. In their perversity and corruption they will not recognise their own incapacity to discover truth, nor receive with gratitude revelations from above; but prefer to trust only to that which their dim, distorted, purblind eyes can *see*. When we contemplate the world from their point of view, we see it, not commingled with the rest of the universe and with heaven, but thrust, as it were, by sin out of its orbit into cold and darkness. Instead of being flooded with light and glory from God's throne, it seems as if the earth were placed under a dome of brass, through the crevices of which only an occasional ray can penetrate. The great mass of the people are contented with this state of darkness and with the swinish indulgences which lie within their reach; but a few are tormented by a desire to look beyond the over-shadowing dome into the infinite beyond. The blind conjectures which they hazard are formed into systems of what they call ' Philosophy,' while their equally futile and crude endeavours

Revolt of the Horses

to understand external nature — into the workings of which we see directly—they call ' Science.' But all their efforts are frustrated by the feebleness of their minds, which may be compared to the fragments of a mirror which can only reflect the minutest objects, and which distort what they reflect. Their utter incapacity for grasping the truth is clearly manifested by the fact that, in every age, new and contradictory theories respecting their own origin and destiny are broached and accepted. For a time, as I have said, they seemed inclined to accept the revelation of the Saviour sent them from above. But His doctrines and precepts were so ill-suited to the dull, vile nature of the Yahoos that they are now turning again for instruction and guidance, even in spiritual matters, to these philosophers and men of science. After the infinite labour and research of many generations, their popular teachers have at last arrived at the conclusion that there is no God, and no future state for the soul ; that man is descended from the ape and will die like a dog. Their poets, too, who once drew their inspiration from above, and dreamed and sang of heaven, are now, for the most part, atheists or sensualists, who believe in nothing but what they call the laws of matter, which they invent and change at pleasure. Always miserable enough, they have been now brought by such theories to such depths of ignorance and despair as to ask 'whether life is worth living!'

Revolt of the Horses

"You will naturally ask how a tribe of Yahoos, such as I have described, who are not subjugated and controlled by a higher race, can, when left to themselves, continue to exist at all. I have said that though there is no real distinction of classes founded on actual physical or intellectual superiority, their pride incites them to set up all kinds of artificial barriers. The chief distinction is the possession of what they call 'wealth.' Anyone who possesses this is further distinguished by some name, which gives him a claim to the homage and services of others, and entitles him to look down upon them as inferiors. Those who cannot get wealth seek to raise themselves above the vulgar mass by the acquisition of what they call 'learning'—*i.e.* the knowledge of the false theories and absurd opinions of men of former generations. By means of this knowledge and the power of persuasion generally connected with it, and which they call 'eloquence,' they are able to induce the more ignorant and weak-minded to submit to their rule, to supply them with the means of indulging their appetites and their vanity. Knowing, or pretending to know, a little more than others, they contrive by skilful lies to make them do what they wish, and even prevail on the wealthy to give them a share of their good things. When these 'clever' Yahoos are unable to gain the favour of the wealthy, they pretend to be friendly to the 'lower class,' and incite them to plunder their richer neighbours.

"Singularly enough, in this land and among this

Revolt of the Horses

tribe, which, vile and degraded as it is, is universally acknowledged to be the least corrupt of the human race, the external forms of rational government still exist. Like ourselves they have, nominally at least, the institution of monarchy, but, incredible as it may seem to you, the monarch and his family are not distinguished from the rest of the tribe by superior size, or strength, or beauty, by any greater moral or intellectual gifts, or by sublimity of soul; although it must be confessed that examples of the highest excellence attainable by a Yahoo have appeared among the sovereigns, and especially among the female sovereigns of this land. The chief benefits of kingship, therefore, are wanting. Yet, no doubt, it once had the advantage of affording a centre of union; and the strong hand of the monarch kept the unruly creatures in some degree of order. But few Yahoos can possess power without abusing it, and employing it principally for their own selfish ends. The same may be said of the aristocracy, which, like ourselves, they also have; but here, too, only in name, since its members are not distinguished from the rest of the nation by physical perfection or spiritual insight. Their rule, too, while it lasted, had certain advantages. Being exempted from all bodily labour they had time to learn the art of government, and to form less filthy and disgusting habits than the common herd. The exercise of power gave them the confidence and courage necessary to dominate so turbulent and quarrelsome a tribe. But here

Revolt of the Horses

again the corruption and ineradicable selfishness of the Yahoo nature led them to oppress their meaner fellows, and to monopolise too great a share of the means of life. Monarchy and aristocracy having failed, the attempt is now being made to govern this miserable country according to the whims and vagaries of the lowest and most ignorant of the people ; apparently with the idea that matters may be mended by placing folly and weakness in the seat of power, as assessors of selfishness and sin. The sceptre of authority has been wrested from the hands of kings and nobles—who, at anyrate, *did* rule and keep something like order among these brutes— and is now tossed about from one unclean hand to another by those who succeed for a time in cajoling the multitude by eloquent flattery and plausible lies. It is indeed a piteous spectacle to see this miserable horde of Yahoos, destitute of the wisdom or the courage to find its own path through life, staggering about in the quagmire of misery and corruption, in pursuit of some oratorical will-of-the-wisp, and continually sinking deeper and deeper in the slough of despond."

CHAPTER VIII

MEANWHILE, the mind of Hippophil was perplexed by the difficulties consequent on what
was regarded as the failure of the Prince in the
trial gallop. Baby Ned, who had conceived a
personal animosity against both Aethon and
Hippophil, denounced the former as a "bolter,"
of bad temper, impossible to ride; and entirely
destroyed his character as a candidate for racing
honours. Ned himself broke off all connection
with Lord Pevensey. Hippophil, however, did
not give up the idea of entering the young
Houyhnhnm for the Derby, as the presence on
that occasion of many of the highest order of
horses, and of the *élite* of the Yahoo tribe, would
form a favourable opportunity for the outbreak
of the revolt. He therefore cast about for
another rider, over whom he might exercise
complete control, and who would implicitly obey
his instructions in regard to the treatment of
the Prince. His attention had been attracted
to one of the junior grooms in Lord Pevensey's
stables, not only by his good seat and light hand,
but by his judicious and gentle treatment of the
horses under his charge. This boy, Will Pinder
by name, had witnessed the catastrophe at the
trial, and Hippophil had heard him remark in a

low voice that "it was all Ned's fault, and that it was no good bullying a sensible horse like that." After a good deal of talk with him, Hippophil one day asked him whether he would like to be trained as a jockey. Will replied, with modest surprise, that this had always been his dream, but that no one had a chance of entering what was practically a close corporation, unless he were a member of some well - known jockey family, or was lucky enough to be taken up by some influential trainer.

" I 've as much chance of getting a good horse to ride in a race as of being Lord Mayor of London."

Hippophil then took the first opportunity of broaching the subject to Lady Ermyntrude, with whom he stood in great favour on account of his devotion to the Prince, and who had also noticed Will as superior to his fellows in the stables. She promised to mention him to her father, and to ask him to have the boy trained. Lord Pevensey was highly amused at seeing his gentle, modest girl interesting herself in races and jockeys, but saw no reason to refuse, even had he ever been able to deny a wish of hers. He was, however, firmly convinced that the Prince was impossible as a Derby runner, and ridiculed the notion of a raw lad managing a horse which had dismissed the redoubtable Ned from his back. He consented to speak to his trainer, Mr Horrock, and the latter made no objection, but laughed heartily at the thought of Will's

Revolt of the Horses

riding such an animal at the Derby, and said : "The boy or the devil may ride him for all I care, but there's one that won't ride him anywhere, and that's me." Lady Ermyntrude was highly displeased at this insult to her favourite, and was only pacified by her father's assurance that if Hippophil consented she might have her pet for her "right own," and run him for the Derby if she pleased, but that she could hardly do so in her own name.

Hippophil explained the state of matters to Aethon, and Will was introduced into the stable of the dower-house to attend on him under Hippophil's superintendence. It was understood that neither whip nor spur was to be used, and that pace was to be regulated by the voice alone. Will was greatly astonished at the attitude of Hippophil towards the Prince, but he was himself very soon inspired, by his majestic bearing, with a somewhat similar feeling of reverence. Several secret trials were made by the young jockey in presence of Hippophil alone, and the former was soon convinced of what the latter knew already, that the Prince could, with the greatest ease, maintain a pace for the longest distance far beyond any recorded in the annals of racing. This conviction having been obtained, Aethon was relieved from all further annoyance, and allowed to range freely through the park, and to mature his plans for the coming revolution.

Their first care was to form an estimate of the degree in which the complicated machinery of human life depended on the labour of horses. The time was not long past when the entire transport of the country was carried on by means of horses. Now, however, the great bulk of this work was effected by steam, electricity, and other agencies. But still the number of horses employed was not diminished, and the sudden withdrawal of their labour would, even now, throw everything out of gear. The railways were indeed the main arteries of the body politic, but the horses were still the veins and nerves of the nation's life. Food, clothing, and all the myriad necessaries of human existence might be conveyed in the mass by steam to a few great centres; but their distribution could only be effected by the incessant labour of horses. Without them the land could not be efficiently tilled, nor the cargoes of food from abroad, on which England had become dangerously dependent, discharged and warehoused. In a still greater degree than in the towns, the inhabitants of the remoter parts of the country were dependent on horse-transport for their necessary supplies. The Prince, therefore, came to the conclusion that a strike of the horses would go far to paralyse the social system, and reduce the nation to a helpless mass of confusion, and must soon lose all vitality. The chief advantage of the Yahoos in an open conflict lay, as Hippophil suggested, in the extraordinary perfection to which they had brought the science and art of destroying life. For this object the greatest expenditure was, in all ages, incurred; and not only were the strongest men qualified by laborious training for the task of killing and mutilating one another, but by far the greatest portion of the intellect and inventive genius of mankind was directed towards the same object. Unarmed Houyhnhnms and horses could not stand for any length of time before the terrible artillery of these cunning and bloodthirsty Yahoos. A direct conflict, therefore, must, as far as possible, be avoided, and every means employed to destroy the weapons and the powder with which they were charged. The great depôts of these materials of war might be ascertained and watched, and, if possible, their contents destroyed or scattered. Happily, the mighty engines of destruction could only be moved from place to place by horses. The chief hope of the Houyhnhnm Prince, however, lay in the disturbance of all social arrangements, by which the greater number of Yahoos would be starved to death; the rest, he thought, would probably fall victims to an internecine struggle for the possession of the inadequate supply of food. No doubt, as Aethon said, the horses would be called on to brave the most terrible dangers, and to meet suffering and death in every form. But what was that to them —to the martyr-race—whose whole life was made up of imprisonment, exhausting labour, disease, and torture? Were they not exposed to these same infernal weapons in the service of Yahoo riders, and forced into unnatural conflict with their fellow-horses? Was not every battlefield covered with their shattered limbs, and whitening bones? What could await them worse than that which they already suffered, without purpose and without hope?

The general plan of the revolt was this: On the appointed day every horse throughout the kingdom, when led out to be harnessed or groomed, was to break away from the hands of his attendants, repair to a common centre, and place himself under the orders of a chief appointed by the Prince. The horses belonging to a city or town were to assemble at one or more places outside the walls, and either destroy or drive in all the Yahoos whom they found in the fields. If the latter, on recovering from their consternation, should come forth with rifles in their hands, the horses were to retreat out of range, unless their leaders saw a chance of overpowering the enemy by a sudden charge. After a time, the Yahoos must retire from exhaustion or want of food; then the horses should return to their former position, surround the town or village, and destroy all those who attempted to escape. In the larger towns, it was hoped, the Yahoos would aid the movement by internal dissensions, since the common people, finding themselves without work or food, would naturally lay the fault on the upper classes, and rise against them. Having plundered and massacred the rich, the people would then divide themselves under their party chiefs and orators, and in their deadly strife soon use up their supply of ammunition. When

Revolt of the Horses

this was done, the remnant might easily be destroyed by a rapid charge. The chief attention was to be directed to London, the heart and brain of the nation, to which, on the outbreak of the revolt, thousands would resort from all parts of the country. The very crowding of the metropolis, however, would greatly promote the success of their enterprise, because it would increase the number of mouths to be fed on the rapidly diminishing supply of food, and would add fuel to the fires of civil war.

As soon as the disaster which had befallen England became known to the rest of the world, large supplies of food would naturally be brought into her ports by foreigners, hoping to make enormous gains out of the necessities of the starving people. But the want of horses would retard all distribution, and the transport by human labour alone might be greatly impeded by the horses.

There could be little or no doubt that the effects of the strike would be felt throughout the whole fabric of society, which was almost entirely based on the slave labour of horses. The entire occupation of a large section of the richer Yahoos consisted in riding, hunting, and racing horses. Their strength was used to draw the female Yahoos, enfeebled by luxury and idleness, from place to place. Without horses they would be deprived of their greatest pleasure, that of displaying their wealth and exciting the envy of their neighbours. Without horses they could

Revolt of the Horses

attend no feasts or balls; there would be no fox-hunts, no races; and life would lose all its interest and charm in the eyes of the richest men and women. On the other hand, hundreds of thousands of the lower class were employed in tending horses, in preparing food for them, in working with them in various ways; and all these would be suddenly left without occupation and wages. In sum, therefore, it seemed to the Prince that the main work of destroying the Yahoos would be speedily and effectually performed by the Yahoos themselves.

CHAPTER IX

IN the year 1951 the sporting world in England
was in a state of more than usual excitement,
owing to the unprecedented number and excellence of the horses entered for the Derby, and
the apparent equality of several among them.
The meeting was likely also to be a remarkable
one for its international character. England, at
this period, had fallen very low in the scale of
nations, and the remembrance of her former
supremacy, though not sufficient to rouse her
people to any sustained effort to regain it, seemed
to incite foreign nations to try and surpass her,
even in the most trifling pursuits in which she
had formerly led the van. "It is quite extraordinary," said a foreign diplomatist of the day,
"how difficult it is, even now, to beat out of
John Bull's thick head the idea that he is cock
of the European walk!" Egypt had been lately
given up to the French, and Gibraltar to the
Spaniards; and the Russians were making rapid
progress towards the conquest of India. Enchanted by their easy victories in diplomacy, in
gaining which they had received the most valuable assistance from political parties in England
herself, they found a further delight in beating
her on her own racecourse, in her own national

Revolt of the Horses

and favourite pastime. Many of the best horses had been bought at fabulous prices by wealthy Irish-Americans, Frenchmen, and Russian nobles ; and had it not been for a few men like Lord Pevensey, or a Birmingham millionaire, no colt of any pretension would have fallen into English hands. The favourites were :

Mr O'Brien's	. .	Home Rule.
Lord Tweedledee's	.	Socialism.
M. Paul Vairon's	.	Cairo.
Prince Kolticoff's	.	Herat.
Lord Pevensey's	.	⎰Ladas. ⎱Lois.

Among the entries was—

Mr Hippophil's . . Houyhnhnm Prince, which attracted some notice, because no mention was made of either sire or dam, and few in racing circles, to which Swift was utterly unknown, had ever heard of the Houyhnhnms.

Racing, like poverty, makes one acquainted with strange bedfellows. It would be difficult to find a more incongruous company than that which was drawn together by one common taste at the hospitable table of Sir Robert Denham of Pyecroft House — a neighbour of Lord Pevensey's—a man who lived for the turf alone, and was supposed to have lost and won more money on horses than any man in Europe.

In appearance he was of the " aristocratic type," so rare in aristocratic families. He had a graceful but strong and well-knit frame, slightly above the middle height, a small head with high but

Revolt of the Horses

narrow forehead, a moderately high nose, short, well-cut upper lip, large brown eyes, which looked like the special love-gift of a beautiful mother, and black hair just sprinkled with the frost of his fiftieth year. The expression on his face was one of impenetrable calm, and showed no change, even when the number of the Derby winner was run up or his favourite racer began to cough. His education was of the usual kind. He had passed through school and university without any marks of the passage, except, perhaps, an easy *savoir vivre*. But though he had received no education, he had educated himself in all that seemed to him worth knowing. He knew every bone and muscle, every artery and vein in a horse's body. He was an excellent veterinary surgeon. He knew the stud-book by heart. In history he knew the particulars of every important race that had taken place in England, and could repeat the name of every winner of every important event, and those of their owners and riders. In geography his knowledge was chiefly confined to the racing centres of England ; but he knew Paris, Baden-Baden, and a few other Continental towns. His knowledge of mathematics was circumscribed but deep, for he could make a book, the intricate calculations of which would have puzzled a senior wrangler. His "stud-mare," as he sometimes called his wife, was a tall, handsome, gentlemanlike woman, who had distinguished herself as a horsebreaker, and as a splendid

Revolt of the Horses

rider at Islington, and "to hounds." The other guests, some of whom were staying in the house, were Lord Pevensey, Mr Ellersley-Bignall, Radical M.P. for the county, Lord Tweedledee, Socialist peer, Mr O'Brien, the Irish-American, several local magnates, owners of racers, and last but not least, and by special favour, Baby Ned the jockey, who had lately transferred his services to Sir Robert Denham. It was properly a gentlemen's party, and nothing would have induced her father to bring Lady Ermyntrude. But exceptions were made in favour of the hostess, Lady Denham, and her intimate friend the Marchioness of Hampshire, a well-known turfite, whose sex seemed to be an absurd freak of Nature; and who, in her language, tastes, and pursuits, was essentially a *man* of the coarest type, "only more so." Not that she was entirely without some feminine weaknesses, for although she had no attractions for men, they had considerable attractions for *her;* and although she was on the wrong side of sixty and of an unwieldy barrel-shape, from excessive indulgence at table, she still hoped, by painted eyebrows, false teeth, a rakish wig, and a liberal use of rouge and pearl powder, to repair the ravages of time, and attract the regard of the other sex. The dinner was the result of the most consummate culinary skill brought to bear on the finest materials which Nature can produce. The conversation turned, in the first place, on the race meeting of the approaching season, the qualities of the horses,

Revolt of the Horses

and the state of the betting-market, on which Baby Ned was a great authority. But pleasure was combined with business; and all the scandals of the last season were warmed up again, and many a *risqué* anecdote was told, with the full consent of the Marchioness, who, when she saw any faltering on the part of the narrator, as he drew near the point of his tale, said, with encouraging frankness, "Remember, you may tell *me anything*."

During a pause in the conversation, Baby Ned, who, although he had left Longwood in dudgeon, was by no means minded to cut Lord Pevensey, asked him whether he knew anything of the horse entered under the name of the " Houyhnhnm Prince" and owned by a Mr Hippophil. "Was not that the name of the man I saw at your place, when I rode that queer brute in your park."

"Yes," said Lord Pevensey, coldly; "and my friend Mr Hippophil is here."

"Oh," said Ned, addressing him, "I beg pardon, but do you really mean to run that beast at the Derby?" Hippophil, who was annoyed by the half-sneering tone of the question, replied stiffly in the affirmative.

"Well," said Ned, " I admire your pluck. You won't get any of *us* to ride him. I would myself as soon mount a two-year-old zebra. But if you'll give me your word that he is to run, I'll give you twenty-to-one against him in any coin you please."

"Very well," said Hippophil, quietly—"ponies."

Revolt of the Horses

This conversation drew the attention of the other guests, and the Marchioness insisted on Ned giving her a full description of the Houyhnhnm Prince.

"Well, my lady," said Ned, "I won't deny that the animal we're speaking on is as fine a picter of a 'orse as ever was foaled, with the softest skin, the deepest shoulders, the fullest haunches, the cleanest shanks, the finest, flattest legs, and full-bloodedest head, and eyes like blazing coals; and my eye! what a muzzle! Why, he could drink out of a tumbler! But he's got no pedigree to show, and no training. He's a buck-jumper and a bolter, and no more fit to race than a Highland stag."

Lord Pevensey quoted the lines of Hurdis:

"Give me the steed
Whose noble efforts bore the prize away;
I care not for his grandsire or his dam."

But in the eyes of the others Ned's judgment settled the matter, and the same odds were offered from several quarters, which Hippophil accepted to the amount of £20,000 to £40,000. Lord Pevensey was silent, and seemed annoyed at the mention of the horse. The Irish-American, O'Brien, though he made a small bet with Hippophil, rather hung back, and seemed much struck by Ned's description of Aethon. The Frenchman, Paul Vairon, was ready to bet against him to any amount.

"I suppose," said the hostess, "that Mr Hippophil knows *something* about his own horse;

126

Revolt of the Horses

where he was bred, and from what strain he comes."

Hippophil coldly replied that he had no information to give, and that the horse came into his possesion by accident.

"I should like," continued Lady Denham, "to see an animal that no one can ride; perhaps some day you will let *me* try him."

"For heaven's sake," said Ned to Hippophil, "don't do anything of the kind. It would be suicide on her ladyship's part and murder on yours. Although," he added, "I must confess that your ladyship would have a great advantage over us, for the brute has one good quality—he's a great admirer of beauty; and the only person who can do what she likes with him, as Lord Pevensey will tell you, is the Lady Ermyntrude."

"Really," said the Marchioness, bridling and smiling, "I feel quite interested in this extraordinary creature. I shall certainly drive over to Longwood to-morrow, and, if you will allow me, take a look at him."

A dead and very significant silence followed this announcement, and glances were exchanged not flattering to her ladyship. However, on the following day, she drove up to the dower-house at Longwood, and went with Hippophil into the stable of the mysterious racer, accompanied by several of the Longwood party. When the Marchioness looked through the rails of the loose-box, the prince was standing quite still in deep thought, with his head turned away from her.

Revolt of the Horses

On hearing footsteps he turned round, and seeing a person in female dress, mistook her in the dim light for Lady Ermyntrude, and moved towards her. Encouraged by his quiet and gentle manner, the Marchioness entered the box and extended her hand to caress him. A glance at her face revealed his error to the Prince, and, stopping suddenly, he snorted violently, while a look of intense disgust flashed from his proud eyes; then wheeling round on his hind legs, he sprang with a bound to the farthest and darkest corner of his box, averting his head, as if to shut out the sight of Yahoo deformity in its most hideous aspect. The Marchioness, in mortal terror, flung herself out of the box, and was received with an uncontrollable burst of laughter by her unsympathising friends and the broad grins of the stablemen, which, had she not been so well rouged, would have made her white with fury. Her language became unparliamentary. "D——d brute!" she said. "I wonder, my Lord Pevensey, that you keep such a wild beast in your stables." Having further vented her wrath in language which filled the stable boys with the keenest delight, she returned to Pyecroft, shut herself up in her own rooms, and was seen no more that day. Her discomfiture was a delightful source of conversation and mirth at the dining-table and in the servants' hall; and all agreed that the Houyhnhnm Prince was "no bad judge."

On the following day the company dispersed, and spread the opinions entertained of the

Revolt of the Horses

in various directions. The betting against him was generally up at twenty-five to one. By Hippophil's advice Lord Pevensey took these odds to a considerable amount, though without any strong conviction, and laughingly told his daughter that if her ill-behaved darling won, she should have the stakes, which would add some £30,000 to her dowry.

Soon after his return to Longwood, Hippophil received a visit from the Irish-American, O'Brien, whom he had met at Pyecroft, and who now requested to be allowed to see the Prince stripped. Hardly knowing what reason to give for refusing, Hippophil went to consult Aethon. They agreed to admit the American, but Hippophil begged the Prince to keep up his character for ill-temper. No sooner, therefore, had O'Brien entered the loose-box, than Aethon threw up his heels and rushed at him with open mouth, and with indignation, not altogether feigned, flashing from his eyes. O'Brien had just time to escape. "Confound him," he said, shaking himself, "he's a dangerous lunatic. I hadn't even time to study his points; but points or no points, nobody can ride him, and he's well out of the running." Hippophil was rejoiced to get rid of him so easily; but on the following day he saw a man crouching behind a hedge, by the side of which Aethon was accustomed to pass in his daily gallop. Suspecting a spy, Hippophil accosted him sharply, and had his suspicions confirmed by the man's sheepish manner and evasive answers. He therefore warned the Prince

Revolt of the Horses

to keep as far away as possible from the public thoroughfares, and, if seen, to deepen the impression of his uncontrollable violence of temper.

Aethon had frequent opportunities of following this advice. The extraordinary language of Ned the jockey respecting the splendid qualities of "the wild horse," whose savage temper alone he had been able to denounce, produced a great impression on the party at Pyecroft; and curiosity, whetted by self-interest, was rife among them. Spies made their way into Longwood Park, and watched for hours in hopes of getting a fair view of the "dark horse without a pedigree." On one occasion an envoy, bolder than the rest, came towards him as he was advancing slowly down the avenue, and held out a sieve of corn, at the same time addressing him in a wheedling tone. The Prince allowed him to come within a few yards, and then suddenly jumped right over his crouching form. The man took to his heels in mortal terror, and just managed to escape the pursuing Houyhnhnm through a thorn hedge, on which he left a considerable portion of his clothing. He revenged himself by hurling a few stones and a great many curses at the Prince as he moved slowly away, but from that time forward the persecution ceased, and the park was as sacred to him as his meadow to a savage bull.

When the Houyhnhnm missionary could divert his thoughts from the degraded and suffering creatures of his own blood, he interested himself

Revolt of the Horses

in the study of the strange race which resembled
so closely the Yahoos of his own land, and yet,
in many points, differed so widely from them. He
learned much from frequent conversations with
Hippophil, but he was not without many opportunities of studying human nature by actual
observation of those about him. Scarcely a day
passed by in which Lord Pevensey did not spend
an hour or two in the stable, in the company of
the rector of the parish, or of visitors at Longwood,
among whom were not only eminent sportsmen,
but occasionally men of the highest rank in the
political, literary, and social worlds. The conversation to which he listened on all kinds of
subjects excited, in the highest degree, his amused
astonishment. Filled as he himself was with the
light of reason and truth, he looked with pitying
sadness on the blind wanderings of their minds,
the feeble groping of their weak hands after
heavenly treasures. What astonished him most,
perhaps, was the mixture of good and evil in the
same person. He could not but recognise in Lord
Pevensey many noble qualities—honour, integrity,
patriotism, and a real desire to benefit his fellow-
creatures, and to make them happier by his life
and actions. And yet he gathered from his
conversation that he had been often swayed by
the coarsest passions and the meanest motives,
by pride, and greed, and lust, and that self-love
was often the root of his seeming virtues. Others,
again, to whose utterances he listened with disgust
and horror, were openly, cynically bad ; apparently

Revolt of the Horses

without an aspiration beyond the gratification of some sensual desire, or the hope of gaining some advantage which would enable them to set their foot on the necks of others.

These things perplexed and saddened him, and he wondered that either the better spirit within them did not rise triumphant over the sin-poisoned flesh, or that the faint flame from heaven, which still flickered in the bosoms of some of them, was not once for all extinguished by the ever-rising flood of corruption. The slight and infrequent marks of goodness which he saw in the hearts of men were not sufficient, indeed, to alter his opinion of their hopeless corruption, or to divert him from the task of exterminating them; but it rendered that task more painful to him. One person alone, as we have said, had ever inclined him to suspend his judgment, and that was the Lady Ermyntrude. She had always been fond of horses, and had had many a pet, ranging in rank from Shetland pony to thoroughbred lady's hunter; but the Prince had a strange fascination for her, and she never seemed better pleased than when she was smoothing his velvet neck or looking into his lustrous eyes. She was, of course, unable to appreciate the intelligence with which they beamed, but their expression struck her as something as strange as it was beautiful. Her father asked her one day whether she would not like to ride her favourite, who, though he would probably fail as a racer, might be trained as a lady's horse. "He is always gentle enough with you,

Revolt of the Horses

Ermy; and fancy what a sensation he would cause in the Row!"

"I should not be in the least afraid," she said; "and I am sure he would not hurt me; but, oddly enough, I have no longer any desire to mount him. He seems to me too good to be bridled and saddled and hauled and driven about like other horses. I like to see him here in our park, galloping riderless along with his head in the air, and looking as if the whole place belonged to him. No, he is too good to ride. I only wish he could talk to me, which he almost does. I 'm sure he would have plenty to say; just look at his eyes! Are not they really *speaking* eyes?"

Aethon, on his part, continued to be greatly interested in what he considered a phenomenal Yahoo, who seemed to be free from the meanness and vileness of her species. He could not, it is true, altogether overcome his repugnance to her form, so intimately associated in his mind with brute ignorance and depraved instincts; but she was far less distasteful to his delicate sense of the beautiful than any other of the miserable race; nor did her simple, close-fitting dress of blue cloth, with the neat frill round the neck, excite his derision like the extraordinary costumes he had seen on the Marchioness and other women. If the preposterous habit of wearing clothes was to prevail, it assumed in her the least offensive aspect. But what astonished him beyond all measure, and at the same time attracted him, was the purity of her heart, the sweetness of her dis-

133

position, her overflowing affection for all and everything about her. Able as he was to gaze into every recess and corner of her mind, he searched in vain for one mean thought, or base desire, or unkind feeling. He found no pride, no jealousy, no selfishness, but loving devotion to her father, of whom she knew only the best side, and a fond attachment to her home. He saw, too, that her domestic affections, far from taking the usual form of exclusive interest in what immediately concerned herself, were only the brightest manifestations of the universal love with which her heart was overflowing. Her mental vision was, of course, circumscribed and weak, like that of other Yahoos ; but she was, at any rate, free from the load of complicated error by which the intellect of so-called learned men was crammed and stifled. She knew but little of theology, and had probably never heard of the Council of Trent, or the wars of the Utraquists ; but God's Word was a spring of peace and joy to her heart, and she looked forward to the brighter world which it promised her with almost a Houyhnhnm's unclouded faith. She was but very imperfectly acquainted with natural science, with the successive changes by which, according to modern theories, her little person had been evolved during some millions of years out of some slimy matter at the bottom of the ocean. But the warm sunshine, the refreshing breezes, the glad flowers of spring, and the rich tints and fruits of autumn, while they thrilled her senses with delight, brought a deeper joy to her soul, as messages of love and promise from Him, in whose protecting arms she felt herself safe for time and eternity. The Prince was struck, too, by the magic influence which this inexplicable creature exercised on those around her. The conversation between Lord Pevensey and his distinguished visitors was by no means always edifying. Plans for hoodwinking and defeating political opponents, for gaining some petty triumph over social rivals, were freely discussed, with a cynical disregard of moral obligations. The weaknesses and errors of friends and neighbours were enlarged upon with ridicule and keen enjoyment. But in the presence of this young and simple girl the whole atmosphere seemed changed. The cold, censorious man of the world was metamorphosed into the loving father, who saw everything through his daughter's eyes of love and pity. The very stablemen were unconsciously affected by her approach, and the expression of their features and the tone of their voices changed, as if face and tongue had been touched by a passing angel's wing. Few men could see her pass without a quivering of the knee, a desire to kneel and do homage to the might and majesty of loveliness and purity.

She was often made the subject of conversation between Aethon and Hippophil. " How," asked the former on one occasion, "do you account for this strange phenomenon — this purity springing from the heart of corruption? In intelligence and disposition she is on a level with our working

Revolt of the Horses

Houyhnhnms, and were it not for the base form in which that loving, generous heart is shrouded, she might dwell with us in our own dear home. Is she a single instance — a unique miracle in the annals of the human race?"

"No," replied Hippophil; "in that sex, and at that age, such cases, though rare, are not unknown. They are the spots of clear water so often seen in the muddiest streams, and they disappear as rapidly. We seem to see in them the first mother of mankind appearing again to gladden the sad earth, and to shed over it the bright hues of Paradise. But the gleam of light is as transient as it is unspeakably lovely. For awhile the inherited seeds of sin and misery in that young creature's nature seem dead; they are only latent. Father and mother, grandparents and great-grandparents are all there in that little frame, and will surely one day make their presence known."

"Is there no way," said the Prince sadly, after a pause, "of isolating, of preserving her?"

"None," said Hippophil; "none but removal to Houyhnhnm's land or an early death. Where should she go? With whom can she associate? Besides, the enemy is within as well as without. She is bound by her social ties and affections to the sensual and the base."

"But how," urged the Prince, "is this corruption brought about. I see nothing in her mind and heart to warrant your forebodings."

"How," replied Hippophil, "did Eve lose Paradise and all the glory of her innocence and

136

Revolt of the Horses

beauty? The same spirit of evil which tempted her is already looking over the fence which has hitherto guarded this human marvel, and preparing to seize his victim. You have observed," he continued, "that handsome young Yahoo who so often comes here with Lord Pevensey, and who was lately describing how he had ridden his horse to death in a 'glorious run with the hounds'?"

"Yes," said Aethon. "He is the son and heir of Sir Robert Denham," continued Hippophil; "the nearest and most powerful neighbour of the Pevenseys. He is, according to their ideas, beautiful and strong; has a very winning voice and manner, and is especially attractive to the female sex. Well, at the wish of her father, Lady Ermyntrude will give herself up, body and soul, to him, and will invest him with all the bright and glorious faculties and virtues which abound in her own nature. She will adore the idol on which she herself has hung all the attributes that hide its ugliness. And he—he is coarse and brutal in the highest degree; ignorant, vain, and selfish, caring for nothing but his own sensual enjoyments, incapable of a generous thought or noble impulse— utterly untouched by any spiritual influence. He will take her because she is rich and noble, and because her modest loveliness excites his base passions to the utmost. He will pass from the embraces of foul harlots to her pure arms, bringing with him moral corruption and death. For the lofty and lovely qualities of her mind and heart he cares not a jot. She will be indissolubly bound to

Revolt of the Horses

him, and when she discovers that the god of her dreams is a foul idol of clay, she will either die of a shock of moral paralysis, or, more probably, she will try to degrade herself through love for him; the light of heaven will fade from her eyes, and she will blindly, willingly follow her lord and master down the steep of hell. How can she escape when her own father, who loves her, and her own inherited nature, combine to drag her to her doom?"

"But," answered the Prince, "are such natures never found in the other sex, and might she not be united to one as pure and noble as herself? Are there no half-Houyhnhnm beings like yourself?"

"Yes," said Hippophil, "there are such natures among men, but they are *infinitely* rare. And when such happy natures are united, they would be happy indeed were it not that just these very noblest and rarest human beings feel most keenly the 'Weltschmerz,' the misery and corruption of the world around them; and instead of living their own lives, they exhaust themselves in the vain struggle with sin and its attendant evils. And besides, such unions are rendered almost impossible by the complicated and unnatural forms of social life, by the thousand artificial barriers of prejudice and class by which men are separated; and, above all, by the liability even of the best to be deceived by false appearances. Take for example the pair of whom we have been speaking. See them together in a drawing-room—both beautiful and elegant in form and dress (according to Yahoo

138

notions), equally correct for the moment in conversation, discussing the same topics, and expressing the same sentiments and tastes; and yet the one is an angel in human form, and the other is a selfish beast. A few hours later, perhaps, when she is on her bended knees, in the solitude of her chamber, laying open her pure soul before God, and offering fervent prayer with her pure lips for all who are dear to her, for all who err and want and suffer, he will be ranging about, under cover of the night, with the lowest women of the neighbourhood; and, still worse, playfully endeavouring to drag down innocent girls to infamy and death for the gratification of his selfish lust."

"The race is doomed," groaned the Prince; "and if its destruction were not absolutely necessary to the salvation of our brethren, it would perish even more miserably by its own inherent corruption—by the cancer of ineradicable sin."

CHAPTER X

In the work of organising the general revolt, the beginning of which was fixed for the ensuing Derby meeting at Epsom, many unforeseen difficulties had occurred. Some of these arose, not so much from the expected resistance of the Yahoos, as from the state to which long slavery and oppression had reduced the horses themselves. A sufficient number of leaders had been found in the different sections into which the country had been divided by the Prince and Hippophil—which generally corresponded with the electoral districts —to take the command. These leaders were either entirely or very nearly thoroughbred, as it was found that the higher intellect and courage were concomitants of the purer blood. The two highest classes—mostly racers and hunters—were generally in the best physical condition, because their owners housed and fed them better ; not for love or pity for them, but from self-interest. Even these favoured few were often goaded in the race-course or the chase to efforts beyond their strength, and led back to their stables to die of broken hearts. Others, as hunters, were lamed, impaled on stakes, or had their backs broken by careless or incompetent riders, who, in mad rivalry, were ready to sacrifice the noble animal that bore them

Revolt of the Horses

to the vanity of heading others in the chase. Harrowing reports of such cases continually reached the Prince's ears and filled him with sorrow and indignation.

The case of the inferior breeds was far worse. These were in the hands of men whose only object was to squeeze the greatest amount of profit from their labour. It was a common thing, said Hippophil, for the proprietors of coaches to calculate whether it was more profitable to use up their "horseflesh" rapidly, by excessive exertions for a short time, or to prolong their lives by imposing on them only a moderate amount of work ; whether it paid better to feed them well or to stint them in their food. The life of the horses in public conveyances in the great cities was the most deplorable of all. They were hidden away in dark, noisome holes, without fresh air, without opportunities of bathing ; worked until late in the night, and then bedded for a few short hours on rotten straw. The very Yahoos themselves were sometimes moved to pity by the fearful cruelty daily witnessed in the streets, and Hippophil told the Prince that he had often read remonstrances in the public journals, of which he gave the following sample :—

"'Can no one be made responsible for the gross cruelty that is daily inflicted upon London horses? . . . In this damp foggy weather the oily slime, known as London mud, lies an inch deep on every thoroughfare, and over its slippery, treacherous surface the tortured horses have to fight and struggle with their heavy loads. The sight of

Revolt of the Horses

these brave, patient, willing creatures, panting and straining at their traces, their muscles stretched to the utmost tension, their every nerve twitching with terror and pain, and their gentle eyes so full of trouble is a disgrace to a Christian people'; for," added Hippophil, "they still call themselves a Christian people!"

The life of a Houyhnhnm is nearly always the same—about seventy years; that of a horse under the most favourable conditions, forty, whereas the average life of the horse in a public carriage is from eight to ten, the greater part of which is spent in torment.

The inevitable consequences of such treatment continued through many generations has been a deterioration of the race, not only physical but intellectual, and in a very slight degree moral. The leaders reported to the Prince that in many of their humbler brethren the mental power was very weak, not much superior to that of the rude Yahoos who tyrannised over them; that the traditions of their lofty descent was very vague and faint among them, and that they found great difficulty in understanding the scheme for their redemption and restoration. They lacked both hope and courage, and looked forward to nothing better than to plod the weary round of work and suffering till death released them. "What could we do," they say, "against our masters, with their chains and bridles, their whips and spurs, and the crushing burden which they lay upon our backs? Of course we will obey our

Revolt of the Horses

natural leaders—the noble and fortunate ones to whose superior intelligence and wisdom we look up ; but what can it avail *us* to resist ? " Thus spake many ; others were too old or too worn and weak to be of any active service. It was resolved, therefore, to divide the whole mass of horses into active and passive members of the league, and to expect nothing more of the latter than obedience to the summons of their leader on the day of rising. The work and the fighting would be performed by the active members alone.

In the course of their investigation the Prince and Hippophil became acquainted with interesting passages in the history of this branch of the Houyhnhnm race in general, and of the British horse in particular. They learned with a melancholy interest that the bondage of the horse to the cunning Yahoo dated from the remotest ages, and was testified by the earliest sculptures and paintings of the Egyptians and Assyrians. The noblest specimens of the Houyhnhnm in bondage were found in Arabia, where the climate was more like that of Houyhnhnm-land. The inhabitants, too, whether from a dim notion of the superiority of their horses to themselves, or some other cause, have always treated them as companions and friends, have exempted them from all drudgery, for which they use camels or asses, and only used them for parade or war.

How the pure Houyhnhnm blood first found its way into Arabia is not known, but they ascertained that the ancestors of the thoroughbreds, with whom the Prince had formed such close relations, were brought into England towards the end of the seventeenth century, in the reigns of Charles II. and William III. Foremost among these illustrious ancestors were three horses, known to the Yahoos under the names of the "Bryerly Turk," the "Derby Arabian," and the "Godolphin Arabian."

All English turf horses, Hippophil said, were descended from these three, and in these the Prince found the nearest approach to Houyhnhnm gifts and qualities—keen intelligence, undaunted spirit and readiness to do and suffer anything in the cause of freedom. These descendants were appointed as supreme authorities in their respective rural districts. They were assisted by the second class of horses, chiefly employed in hunting, in whose veins circulated a large amount of pure Arab blood. These, too, though somewhat coarser in their form, were full of strength, high mettle, and earnestness of purpose. A sufficient number of thoroughbreds were resident in London, and these took the direction of affairs in that important centre. They could reckon on the services of a splendid array of so-called riding and carriage horses, and of the noble animals trained for the purposes of war, who were doubly precious in their masters' eyes as aids in the destruction of the Yahoos of other lands. In London, too, unhappily were found the greatest number of those whose strength and spirit were ground down by ill-treatment and its consequences—disease and

Revolt of the Horses

mental incapacity; and it was not without grave anxiety that the Prince looked forward to the result of the rising in the capital.

And now the great day was drawing near—great in the eyes of the racing world, as promising to show the finest sport which had been seen for ages—and doubly great in the eyes of the Houyhnhnms, as heralding the first attempt on a grand scale to throw off the degrading yoke of the despised and detested Yahoo. No less than fifty horses had been entered, but the vast superiority of six of these had led to numerous scratchings, and the list was reduced to twenty, among which were the horses we have mentioned above—viz. :

Prince Kolticoff's. . .	Herat,
Lord Tweedledee's . .	Socialism,
Mr O'Brien's	Home Rule,
M. Paul Vairon's. . .	Cairo,
Lord Pevensey's . . .	{ Ladas, Lois,
Mr Hippophil's . . .	Houyhnhnm Prince,

were the most talked of. The first six of these were so evenly matched that the highest authorities were divided and vacillating in their opinion. The name of the Prince was also brought forward, but only to be put aside on the score of ill-temper and inadequate training. While two to one was the greatest odds that could be obtained against any of the six favourites, twenty and twenty-five to one were freely offered against the "dark horse" of his equally obscure owner.

Revolt of the Horses

There were, indeed, a few who had seen the lordly Houyhnhnm striding across the park at Longwood, or had served him in the stable, who were exercised in their minds as to the correctness of the general opinion, and whose expressions of doubt caused a slight reaction in Aethon's favour. Among these was a stable help of villainous antecedents, named Jack Roberts, who had been employed by Lord Pevensey as an extra hand, but was soon dismissed for idleness and brutality. Despairing of finding employment in the same neighbourhood, where he was too well known, he went up to London. It so happened that about three weeks before the Derby meeting he was in a small public-house in Whitechapel, the favourite resort of a low class of grooms and bookmakers. Here he found one Joe Herrick, a former acquaintance, a kind of cross between bookmaker and burglar ; one who was ready to make money in any way but that of honest labour. Joe's profound admiration for the knowledge and cunning of Baby Ned, the jockey, had induced him to follow his lead in betting against the Prince, and to stake his all, and a great deal more, on the issue. The change in the market, therefore, though as yet very slight, had caused him great uneasiness. He was brooding over the subject when he caught sight of Jack Roberts. "Hallo, Jack," he cried, as the latter advanced through the cloud of tobacco smoke, "how did you come here? I thought you was on a job in Wiltshire." "So I was," said Jack, sullenly.

Revolt of the Horses

"Well?" said Joe.

"Well?" said Jack, imitating him, "it didn't suit me, that's all; much too d——d slow for me. A set of tea-and-bream-butter blokes."

"No fun, I s'pose. Any hosses there?" rejoined Joe.

"Yes."

"What sort?"

"Well, there's Ladas and Lois, and a couple of fillies."

"Any good?"

"Oh yes; as good as anything else, I expect."

"Any others?"

"No, nothing to speak on."

"I thought," pursued Joe, "that that dark horse belonging to a cove called Hippophil is kept down there."

"So he is."

"Well, what's *he* like, and why did he stand so plaguy low in the betting?—and why is he rising just now?"

"How should I know?" said Jack.

"Well, what do you think of him?—you've seen him I reckon?"

"Oh yes, I've seen 'im."

"And what do you think of 'im?"

"What do *I* think of 'im?" said Jack sharply, stuffing tobacco into his pipe with his forefinger. "What the 'ell does it signify what *I* think of 'im?—what good will it do *me* to say what *I* think of 'im?"

This was rather a poser for Joe Herrick, fully

recognising as he did that no man could be expected to take the trouble of speaking unless he got something by it. "Ah, well," he said, after a pause, "that's fair enough. What'll you have? I'm game to pay for anything you like to order."

Instead of any other reply, Jack called the barmaid and ordered kidneys and bottled stout. Then, turning to Joe, he said, "I'm a good-natured cove, and I don't mind letting on a bit about that 'oss. Take my word for it. I've a seen 'im a-standin' and a-runnin', and there ain't no 'orse as ever I see that was a patch on 'im for strength and pace. He's as strong as a helephant, and 'as the legs of a stag."

"The devil!" said Joe; "and here have I been and offered the biggest odds against him for a mint o' money; they told me that no one could ride 'im; that's he's got no sire and no training; was it all to do one out of one's money?"

"Well, no! that's true enough—he 'asn't got a sire, and 'e ain't been trained. All I says is, if you *could* ride 'im, and get 'im to spread 'isself, 'ed run right away from an express train."

Joe got up and walked about the room in a state of great excitement. "I don't like it," he shouted—"I don't *like* it. I believe it's a plant. I believe their training 'im on the sly, and have got some d——d fellow who *can* ride him. It's a beastly shame of a swell like Lord Pevensey to try and rob a 'ardworkin' man like me of his money. I'll 'edge, I will." Jack looked on with amused indifference. "I don't know as I should

Revolt of the Horses

'edge if I was you. Baby Ned's not a fool, and 'e couldn't sit on 'im long. I've put my leg over a few devils in my life, but I'm blessed if I'd mount 'im for £500."

Joe was driven half-wild by this contradictory evidence. "But what's a fellow to *do*?" he cried, planting himself in front of Jack and holding out both his arms. "What in the name of blazes am I to do if he *does* win? I shall have to cut and run. If I'm caught I shall be scragged, and if I get away I shall rot in a French gaol."

"Ah!" said Jack indifferently, after a long and comforting pull at the good black stout, "it's a pity one don't know everythink."

"Pity? I should say it *was* a pity! I wish to hell some one would poison his hay, or that he'd run a nail into his beastly foot, up to the head. People don't leave nails about up there, I suppose?" he said, significantly, as a sudden thought crossed him.

"No," said Jack thoughtfully, "I don't know as they do, but they *might*, you know."

"I know somebody as would give a couple of ponies to hear that the brute had gone dead lame a few days afore the Derby," said Joe.

"Do you!" retorted Jack with a sneer. "That somebody isn't you, I expect. I don't think there are many ponies in *your* paddock."

"Well, there ain't," said Joe; "but I'm not the only one; there's many bigger men than me in it."

No more was said, but they understood each other perfectly; and though Jack knew that his companion was a liar and a swindler, he also knew that he meant what he said, and would not dare, for his own sake, to go from his word. Secret intelligence, secret help, were sure to be well paid for. "Well, ta-ta!" said Joe. "If you ever want to see me you'll always find me here at the right time. And, by-the-way," dropping a couple of sovereigns into his hand, "here's something to pay cabs." And with these words he left the room.

In Churton Street, in the extreme east of London, is a small blacksmith's shop, which for very many years has been kept by a clever artisan in iron, named Harding, who in Florence in the sixteenth century would have made himself a name as an artistic iron-worker. Unfortunately his moral qualities were not of the same calibre as his inventive faculties, and he very early lost the confidence and the custom of all honest folk. He found, however, a very lucrative, and by no means uncongenial, exercise for his skill in the service of those whom curiosity induced to visit the houses and the strong-boxes of their neighbours. His powers of invention and his handicraft were very remarkable, and his sets of burglars' tools were masterpieces of variety, suitability, and finish. It was enough to explain your purpose, and old Harding, for a sufficient consideration, would take real pleasure in furnishing you with the means of effecting it. To this great artist Jack Roberts repaired on the following day, and, with perfect confidence in his secrecy, put the question to him—How might a horse be most effectually and most safely lamed? Harding replied that he had—merely to please his own fancy, excited by the approach of the racing season—designed and executed a beautiful little thing which he called a steel-star. It was formed of ten spikes about one inch or one and a half inches long, fixed in an iron ball, from which they stood out like the quills of an angry porcupine. "That's rather a neat and handy thing," said the artist complacently; "easily carried, and easily hidden in the grass or in straw litter. I don't think you'll beat that. Poison was never much good, and is quite played out." Jack Roberts examined several of these stars admiringly, and readily paid the rather high price demanded for them.

The following night found him in Lord Pevensey's park at Longwood. During his short service there he had observed that the Prince in his lonely gallops was wont to pass between two stately elms which stood only a few feet apart, near the artificial water at the foot of the gentle hill on which the mansion stood. Having carefully cut out round thin patches of turf and scooped out the earth, he deposited Harding's masterpieces in the holes and replaced the grass above them. He had nearly finished his task to his complete satisfaction when he was suddenly interrupted by the sound of whispering voices behind him. Gliding behind a bush, he saw through its branches by the bright starlight a man and woman approaching the elm trees, whom he recognised without much surprise as Mr Denham, who often stayed at Longwood, and Mary Woodcroft. As they came nearer he could hear the pleasant voice of the former explaining how devotedly he loved his companion, and assuring her that if she thought that he had ever admired Lizzie Cobbold, or paid her any attention, she was utterly mistaken. He had seen plain girls, but he really thought Lizzie was the plainest he had ever set eyes on. There was but one fine girl in that neighbourhood, and he need not say who *that* was. The couple passed through the trees during this highly satisfactory explanation, and Mary, who was naturally looking on the ground, saw something white on the grass which she picked up and gave to Mr Denham. It was one of Jack's steel-stars which he had dropped in his haste. Mr Denham having more interesting subjects to think of, paid little attention to it, and put it in his pocket, where it was found by his valet, and shown as a curiosity in the servants' hall. The lovers returned towards the village without again passing through the trees, and Jack, after putting the finishing touch to his work, escaped unseen, and returned next morning to London by an early train.

At daybreak on the same morning Hippophil, according to his wont, opened the door of the Prince's stable, and the royal Houyhnhnm issued forth for his morning's canter and his bath in the lake. According to Jack's calculation, he passed through the two elms at full speed, which was suddenly checked by a sharp pain in his off fore foot, caused by the spikes of the steel-star, which had pierced the frog and penetrated to the quick. For the first time in his short life the noble creature felt a wound which paralysed his movements, and it was with some difficulty and at a very slow pace that he managed to crawl home with the star still sticking in his foot. Hippophil, who was on the watch, hastened to meet him, in a state of the greatest surprise and alarm at his slow and laboured movements. On discovering the cause he was filled with consternation, not only at the injury inflicted, but at the revelation of the dangers which surrounded them from spies and enemies, who shrank from no stratagem, however vile, to damage a competitor for racing honours. The impression made on Aethon himself was deep and lasting, and tended greatly to confirm his conviction of the utter depravity of the Yahoo race.

Hippophil immediately made known the circumstances of the outrage to Lord Pevensey, who received the news with the utmost indignation. Lady Ermyntrude was as furious as so gentle a nature could be, and even consulted the family doctor, to the latter's rather offended surprise, about the injury to her favourite. Failing to get the assistance of Dr Wilson, she besought Hippophil to send for the most skilful "vets." of the neighbourhood, and to spare neither trouble nor expense in the service of the suffering

Revolt of the Horses

Prince. Hippophil needed no pressing, but when he informed Aethon that Mr Turnbull, the well-known veterinary surgeon, was coming down from London to inspect his wound, the Prince positively refused to allow him to do so or even to enter his stable. Lady Ermyntrude was in despair, but by the advice of Hippophil she made no attempt to oppose the Prince's will.

Meantime the spot at which the accident had occurred was thoroughly searched by the police, and the steel-star dug out and examined. The similarity to the one found in Mr Denham's pocket was brought to Lord Pevensey's notice, who thereupon questioned his intended son-in-law on the subject. Mr Denham deposed that he had found it during a nocturnal stroll in the park, when he had been unable to sleep. A private hint from some one in the village to the police led to a domiciliary visit at the house of Mary Woodcroft, who at first protested, with a great show of indignation, that she had not crossed the park for months, and *never* was in it at night time. Under cross-examination, however, she at last broke down, and confessed that she had found the star when in company with Mr Denham. Jack Roberts, who was well, and not favourably, known in the neighbourhood, had been noticed by the porters at the railway station, and their testimony as to the time of his arrival and departure directed the attention of the detectives to that worthy as the probable criminal. They were soon upon his track in London.

Revolt of the Horses

The news of the accident to the Prince was quickly bruited abroad, and, of course, with great exaggeration. The slight rise in his quotation was succeeded by a heavy fall, and no one but Hippophil had the courage to take the enormous odds against him, which were freely offered. In fact, no one believed that he could run, and so he quickly passed out of men's minds.

CHAPTER XI

JACK ROBERTS returned to town, rejoicing in the success of his enterprise and the complete secrecy with which, as he thought, it had been carried out. After waiting a few days till the first excitement should have subsided, he repaired to the place in which he had met Joe Herrick, whom he found alone in the back parlour of the "Three Black Crows." "Well," said Jack in a whisper, slapping his friend on the back, "'ave you 'eard the news? What you wanted is some'ow or other come to pass, and the dark 'orse won't spoil your stomach any more—'e'll go on three legs for a month or more."

"So I 'ear," said Joe with a wink. "What a curious thing. I suppose some careless fellow has been leaving nails about; it didn't ought to be allowed."

"I expect so," said Jack; "but 'ow about them ponies?"

"That's all right, old man," said Joe joyously; "you shall have 'em to-morrow about this time, and here's a couple of sovs. on account."

"Hush!" said Jack pocketing the money, as some one entered the room. The new-comer, who looked like a country bumpkin on a holiday,

Revolt of the Horses

wore an old shooting-coat, gaiters, and a red cotton handkerchief twisted loosely round his throat. He greeted our friends in a hearty voice and with a Yorkshire accent. "Good day, gents, I'se coom oop to Lunnun on the spree, and means to see the Derby." Joe smelt a flat, and got interested.

"Ah!" he said, "you'll be nobbling all our tin. We don't much care about you Yorkshire gents, you're so devilish cute about horseflesh."

"How do you know I'se Yorkshire?" said the stranger. "Howsumever, I ain't a-going to deny it. I'm not ashamed of it, and I do think us knows a horse from a cow. But how's t'betting and what's t'tip?"

"Hem!" said Joe, assuming a cold reserve of manner. "I suppose us do know a few; but what us knows us keeps to wereselves."

"Oh, come!" said the Yorkshireman, "you might 'elp a stranger a bit. I'll stand you what you like t'call for." The confederates suffered themselves to be softened, and with steaming glasses of whiskey and water before them, the three were soon amicably engaged in making a book for the countryman, who displayed a well-filled purse.

"By the way," said the latter, suddenly turning and looking Jack in the face, "what's all this they say about a dark 'oss that was to have run in the Derby, and has been lamed by some scoundrel in Longwood Park?" Jack was so taken aback by this sudden thrust that he only

Revolt of the Horses

stared and turned pale. "Whad-yer-mean?" he said at last, recovering himself, in a husky voice. "I don't know nothink of a dark 'orse—and never 'eard 'e was lame."

"All right," said the countryman, "no offence. I thought as 'ow you might know summat about it up here."

"Get out with yer," said Jack furiously. "You'd better go back to Yorkshire, if you can't talk nothing but d——d rot like that. I'm going," he added nervously, turning to Joe. "Are you a-comin', or do you want some more talk with this gent?"

"Oh, stop a bit," said Joe, who was getting alarmed.

"Yes, stop a bit," said the Yorkshireman, who suddenly dropped his assumed accent, and, opening the door, let in two stalwart policemen. "Stop a bit, I've got something to show you," and he pulled out a paper. "I want you to go with me and these gentlemen to talk about the dark horse; I've brought an invitation from a magistrate, who wants you to help him in finding out the owner of this little thing," showing the steel-star, "which he must have lost in Longwood Park."

"No, you don't," said one of the policemen, seizing Jack's right arm as he dropped it into his coat pocket in search of a revolver. "None of *that*, you know."

Joe Herrick meantime affected the utmost surprise. He had never seen the gent before

Revolt of the Horses

to-night — had quite casually met him. Gent seemed quite respectable — probably some mistake—dreadful thing—when did it happen?— hoped the horse was not seriously hurt—extraordinary what people would do to win a bet. On the demand of the detective he gave a false name and address, and hastily backed out of the room, but not before he had received a significant and menacing glance from Jack. However, he was greatly relieved at getting away for the present, and full of hope that he might reap the benefit of the rascally trick, which he had himself suggested, without the drawback of having to pay for it. He almost regretted that he had been so hasty in handing over the two sovereigns.

The investigations at Longwood had revealed to Lord Pevensey not only the crime of Jack Roberts, but also the unworthiness of Mr Denham, to whom he had given free access to his daughter. Man of the world as he was, he was not greatly *surprised* at the young man's backsliding, but he had been inclined to think him rather better than the common run. He was disgusted, too, at his simultaneous worship of the Venus Urania and the Venus Pandemos; and too good a father to sacrifice his darling's happiness to his desire to see her "well settled" in the world. He lost no time in requesting Mr Denham to leave the house at his earliest convenience, and not to return. All intercourse between Longwood and Pyecroft ceased, as Sir Robert Denham and his lady were highly indignant at the treatment their son had received, and at the breaking off of the proposed alliance "on such ridiculously inadequate grounds—*pour si peu de chose.*"

Lord Pevensey found it very difficult to explain to his daughter the reason for young Denham's sudden departure, and contented himself with saying that he had reason to change his opinion of his character. He was glad to find that his daughter's heart was as yet but slightly touched. Lady Ermyntrude learned much more from her lady's-maid, though even *she* dared not explain the matter fully. She managed, however, to convey to her lady's mind that Mr Denham had been flirting with Mary Woodcroft, and this was quite sufficient to check any nascent feeling of regard in Ermyntrude's mind. She was repelled by the thought that a suitor for her hand could so demean himself with a girl like Mary Woodcroft, whom she had tried to befriend, but found to be a self-conceited, coarse-minded, worthless slut.

Yet it was not altogether without a pang that she closed her heart for ever to one who had made himself so agreeable to her, and to all the possibilities which had grouped themselves round his name and person. She was unusually pensive, therefore, when she went as usual after breakfast to seek her favourite, and to condole with him on the wound in his poor foot. She found him in a like state of depression, not from the pain of his wound, which gave him but little uneasiness, but from heart-sickness at the new revelation of Yahoo meanness and corruption. He was standing with drooping head and dimmed eyes in the middle of his box when she entered, and, without the slightest apprehension, threw her arm over his beautiful neck, and kissed him on the cheek. "Dear old boy," she said, patting him; "did they try to lame him—the cruel wretches!" The Prince was less responsive than usual to her blandishments, and found it more difficult than ever to trust in any creature in Yahoo shape. Hippophil soon joined them, and, after delighting Ermyntrude by his vigorous denunciations of the offenders, discussed with her the best means of preventing the recurrence of similar attacks. The free morning gallop and the bath were, he said, absolutely necessary to Aethon's health and comfort; and yet, how could he be protected from the machinations of such unscrupulous enemies? He could answer for the safety of the stable, in which he virtually lived, but more than that was beyond his power. Something might be done, perhaps, by putting on a watch at night as well as in the day, and Ermyntrude promised to get her father's consent to this precaution.

Hippophil had naturally feared, what Jack Roberts and Joe Herrick had so confidently hoped—viz. that the severe wound on the Prince's foot would utterly disqualify him from putting in an appearance at Epsom. He was astonished, therefore, to hear him refer to the coming race as a matter of course, and to see him moving in the park with his usual elasticity and speed. When Hippophil expressed his surprise, Aethon only increased it by saying that he had purposely quickened the healing process in order to be ready for the race. On observing his puzzled look, Aethon asked him what it was that perplexed him.

"You tell me," answered Hippophil, "that you have purposely quickened the healing process of Nature."

"Yes," said Aethon; "does not Nature heal *your* wounds?"

"Certainly," replied Hippophil; "but we know nothing of her methods, and have no control over her operations."

"But," said Aethon, surprised in his turn, "are not those operations guided by reason and according to a well-considered plan?"

"Very much so, indeed," said Hippophil; "the healing and recuperative power, the ψυχή ἰατρική, the *vis medicatrix*, within our bodies is so active, and the methods by which it works are so well directed and efficient, that it is the object of our greatest wonder and admiration; but it lies entirely out of our cognisance and control."

"Have you then," said the Prince, more and more astonished, "two independent intelligences within you?"

"It appears so," said Hippophil. "Our bodies, their growth, their strength and weakness, their

Revolt of the Horses

diseases and their self-healing powers, are mysteries to us. We watch the movement of our corporeal mechanism as something outside ourselves. Some wise and subtle intelligence, which is called by the Germans the 'dark reason' (*dunkle Vernunft*), regulates its operations with unfailing skill and wisdom; but this mysterious power has no connection whatever with what we call our minds."

The Prince was silent for a time, musing with pitying astonishment over this new proof of the incomplete and fragmentary nature of these half-reasoning Yahoos. "And how," said Hippophil, "is it with you?"

"With us," replied the Prince, "there is no such duality of powers—no such divorce between the reason which guides our outward actions, and the recuperative and healing powers which are inherent in our bodies. These are as much under the direct control of thought and will as the attitudes and movements of the body. All are alike under the influence and the absolute sway of one divine power—the sovereign mind which God has placed for a time in our mortal frame. It is therefore a matter of no difficulty for me to hasten the healing process by a strong effort of the mind directed to the wounded part." Hippophil left the presence of the Prince in awe-struck amazement at this new insight into the lofty sphere in which the Houyhnhnm moved, and with a feeling of deep humiliation at the thought of his own feeble powers.

Revolt of the Horses

But though his wound had caused him but little uneasiness, Aethon suffered deeply from the depressing effects of the climate, the chilly gloom of the atmosphere, and, above all, from the sense of loneliness in the midst of the gross ignorance and moral corruption which surrounded him. It seemed to him that, instead of being commingled in one inseparable and glorious whole, as in his own distant home, heaven and earth were here divided by an impassable gulf. The sun for the most part shrouded himself in clouds, as if unwilling to look on the sins and miseries of humanity; the stars, in diminished size, and with cold and feeble light, seemed far removed from all connection and sympathy with man, and only served to chill the beholder with a sense of his own transitory nature and helpless insignificance. The earth appeared to him wan with age, stricken with disease and barrenness, reluctantly and parsimoniously doling out her scanty foliage and shrivelled fruits to the worn and exhausted tiller, and, after a few short months of feeble activity, sinking back exhausted into the gloomy inertia of winter. What a contrast to the joyous prodigality with which she poured forth her spontaneous gifts in the land of the Houyhnhnms!

But even these maladies of external nature might have been tolerable had they not been aggravated by the aspect of terrestrial life, which seemed regulated, not by the law of universal love, but, it might almost be said, by the law of universal hatred. Each animal seemed to pass its life in fear of some other creature, of whom it was the destined prey and victim. And man, the "lord of all," not contented with imbruing his hands in their blood, and devouring their flesh between death and corruption, sought his chief relaxation from toil, his favourite refuge from *ennui*, in destroying the life of some weaker or less cunning fellow-creature. Was he not himself experiencing in his own person the reckless cruelty with which men pursued the grand object of their lives—to obtain, at any cost, some advantage over their fellows—to gain by others' loss and harm?

He could not altogether divest himself of the fear lest *he* too might be at last contaminated by the knowledge of evil which was so continually forced upon him in the tainted air which he was breathing. He felt his faculties growing dimmer with the fading brightness and gladness of his soul. He found it more and more difficult to recall the thrilling raptures, the heavenly communings of his former life, the joyous echoes of which grew fainter and fainter to his mental ear. Should he ever return to that earthly paradise? or was he destined to be the first martyr of his royal race, and only through the gate of death to rejoin his kindred and regain his home?

But the time of action was at hand, and he would not be wanting to his duty. All was arranged as far as possible for the coming revolt, of which the signal was to be the victory of the Prince at Epsom in the race for the Derby.

Revolt of the Horses

The meeting of the year 1951 at Epsom was, as we have said, looked forward to with unusual interest, on account of its international character and the exceptional excellence of the horses engaged. The volume of the betting was altogether unprecedented, and rich and poor, high and low risked their money with unusual recklessness. Political events were disregarded as far less interesting and important; and the enlightened and pacific ministry of the day were left undisturbed in their negotiations for the "graceful concession" of whatever a powerful neighbour might demand *with a threat of war*. The latest cession was that of the Orkney and Shetland Islands, to which last, as was proved by the Prime Minister, we had no real right at all, as they were only held as a pledge for 600 crowns owing to us by Norway.

A week before the Derby the betting stood as follows :—

15 — 8 ag.	Lord Tweedledee's	Socialism.
2 — 1 „	Mr O'Brien's	Home Rule.
2 — 1 „	Prince Kolticoff's	Herat.
3 — 1 „	M. Paul Vairon's	Cairo.
3 — 1 „	Lord Pevensey's	Ladas.
100 — 8 „	„ „	Lois.
1000 —30 „	Mr Hippophil's	Prince.

Lord Pevensey had taken a house near Epsom for himself and his daughter (who, for the first time in her life, developed a taste for the turf), and a party of friends, among whom Hippophil was included. The Prince, with Ladas and Lois,

Revolt of the Horses

who were intimately associated with him in the conduct of the revolt, were carefully conveyed to Epsom by rail, and established in convenient stables. Aethon had a loose-box to himself, in which Hippophil and the boy Pinder passed their whole time, no strangers being admitted — to the great disgust and wrath of the bookmakers. It was decided, however, that the Prince was hopelessly lame, and would probably be scratched at the last moment.

The Derby day was remarkably fine, and the glorious weather, combined with the special attraction of the race, and the increasing devotion to sports and shows (*panem et circenses*) which generally marks the decadence of a nation, all combined to draw together a fabulous number of spectators. The assembly in the grand-stand and the adjacent lawns could hardly be called "aristocratic" — for few of the nobles or gentry had retained enough of their former wealth to make much show—but it was eminently gorgeous. Pre-eminent by the splendour of their equipages and costumes were the millionaires from Africa and South America, some wealthy bankers from Paris, Vienna, and Berlin, and the great democratic ministers and orators of the day in England. Beauty abounded in all directions, and was *not* hidden under a bushel. As usual, however, on such occasions the most beautiful were not most *en evidence* or the most popular. Lady Ermyntrude, in her unconscious, retiring innocence and quiet dress, was comparatively unnoticed beside the

Revolt of the Horses

gorgeous charms of the professional beauties, tricked out in the last creation of the eccentric imagination of some theatrical favourite or æsthetic man-milliner.

Conspicuous among the four-horse drags, for the beauty of its team and the splendour of its female occupants, was that of Lord Tweedledee, which rivalled that of O'Brien, the Irish American, and that of Guttêres, the Mexican mine owner. Lord Tweedledee's horse, as we have said, was one of the greatest favourites, and the owner had made a tremendous book in the full assurance of winning. Beyond the magic circle of the *millionaire* drags, hundreds of vehicles of a humbler kind fringed the racecourse on either side ; while thousands of pedestrians covered the plain, enjoying the fine weather, the *al fresco* lunch, and the anticipation of the coming sport. The immense number of horses, by which a part of the crowd had been transported to Epsom, were detached from their vehicles and tethered, under the care of some hangers-on of the racecourse. Sounds of riotous mirth were heard in every direction, and all kinds of instruments were being played on at once. These, with the loud discordant cries of the bookmakers, in blue and yellow hats of enormous dimensions, the perpetual motion of the crowd, and the general rush and hurry which reigned in every quarter, made the scene a regular Babel of confusion—a *Walpurgis-nacht* by day. A select number of owners, trainers, and jockeys were assembled in the paddock arranging preliminaries,

168

and subjecting the competing horses to a close and critical examination.

Never, perhaps, was a finer set of thoroughbreds collected in the same narrow space, and almost all looked "fit" and trained to the very hour. Lord Tweedledee's Socialism (we quote from *The Sporting Gazette*, 1951), was a large, red chestnut horse, with a golden coat and magnificent shoulders; but his hind quarters were comparatively poor, and the drooping tail had a mean effect. O'Brien's Home Rule was a small mare, rather too light in the middle piece, but with fine clean legs. The expression of her eyes was uneasy, and bespoke alternately boldness or nervous timidity. Prince Kolticoff's Herat was a whip-cord sort of horse, hard as nails, full of muscle, but with an ugly head. The French mare, Cairo, though known to be good, would not stand picking to pieces. Forehead and eyes were fine, but she had a ewe neck, and was too upright in her pasterns. The best of Lord Pevensey's horses, Ladas, was particularly admired for his splendid quarters and almost faultless proportions, and rose rapidly in the betting after the scrutiny. His stable companion, Lois, a beautiful filly, though very fast for a short distance, could not be relied on as a stayer, and her principal task was to make the running for Ladas.

When the Prince was led in by Hippophil and the young jockey, Pinder, a loud murmur of mingled surprise and admiration rose from the spectators, some of whom, in spite of Hippophil's

Revolt of the Horses

warnings, proceeded to take him by the jaws, or pass their hands down his legs in the usual way. One of these gentlemen found himself suddenly seized by the collar of his coat and lifted into the air; another received one of those lightning one-legged kicks peculiar to thoroughbred horses. With these preliminaries, the Prince cleared the space about him by launching his heels in all directions. Though this tumultuous manifestation of contempt and disgust caused considerable consternation, it was exceedingly welcome to the great majority of those who were interested in the race, and dispelled the fears of many whom the magnificent appearance of the supposed lame horse had filled with dismay.

"Ha! ha!" cried Baby Ned, delighted, "I told you so. The brute's a man-eater. I shouldn't like to be starter; if you wait for 'im, you'll never get your 'orses off in a month of Sundays. 'E'll be over the ropes before 'e gets fifty yards. And who's going to ride 'im?"

"I am," said Will Pinder, modestly.

The crowd laughed, and Ned, looking at him with a sneer, said: "Well, good-bye, then; I'm sorry for your poor mother—excuse a tear. *I* know 'is little game. 'E very near sent *me* to kingdom-come, and I'd sooner ride a bison or an alligator."

"All right," said Pinder, "you 'aven't got to ride 'im; and if 'e does for me, you'll have to do without me."

"Well, we'll *try*," said Ned, viciously. The

170

Revolt of the Horses

chaff from all sides grew fast and furious, but the Prince suffered no more from the delicate attentions of gentlemen sportsmen ; and, in spite of the admiration he excited, he went back in the betting more and more.

The twelve horses who came up to the scratch were among the principal leaders of the revolt, and they found occasion to confer with the Prince, as supreme director, and with the general mass of horses high and low. It was noticed at the time, and well remembered afterwards, that almost all the horses on the course, and especially the racers, kept up a perpetual neighing. The whole air was full of it, to the utter astonishment of the jockeys and grooms, and to the great amusement of the crowd.

According to the Prince's orders, each horse was to do his best in the race, and to act exactly as he would have done under ordinary circumstances. Everything was to be avoided which might excite suspicion. On the conclusion of the race for the Derby, all the horses on the course were to rid themselves of their riders or attendants, gather round their respective chiefs in the centre of the plain, and there form themselves into different troops or regiments. One detachment was to proceed to the railway station and disperse the employés, so as to disorganise the traffic. Other detachments, under the selected leaders, were to gallop off towards the different centres in the south of England, taking with them all the horses whom they found on their route. Finally, they

Revolt of the Horses

were to establish themselves in camps outside the towns designated to them as headquarters, confine the inhabitants to their walls, and prevent all communications with other parts of the kingdom. Aethon himself, with a chosen staff of thoroughbreds, was to gallop off to London, where the horses would be found in full revolt on Hampstead Heath. To this place delegates from all parts of the kingdom were to repair, report what had been done in their respective districts, and confer with the supreme leader of the rebellion. Where it could be done, telegraph wires were to be destroyed, and obstacles placed on the railways. All magazines of powder, stores of arms, etc., were to be carefully noted and watched, and, as far as possible, isolated.

It had been a matter of great concern to Hippophil, and even to the Prince, that Lord Pevensey and his daughter would probably be involved in the suffering and penalties of the whole Yahoo nation. They were both present at the race, and, unless exceptional measures were adopted, they would be immediately exposed to the greatest peril. Hippophil was sincerely attached to both, and especially to Lady Ermyntrude, from whom he had received the greatest kindness. The Prince had been freed by them from all labour and annoyance, and the purity and sweetness of Lady Ermyntrude, and the constant interest she had shown in his welfare, had deeply affected his generous nature, and made him almost forget that she belonged to the odious race—the tyrants

Revolt of the Horses

and tormentors of his brethren. It was arranged, therefore, that the carriage horses of Lord Pevensey should for the present submit to his servants, and that Hippophil should escort him and his daughter to their house near Epsom, and to London, and ultimately provide them with the means of leaving the country in safety.

CHAPTER XII

THE bell now rang for saddling, and the course was cleared. Hippophil in a low voice besought the Prince to have patience and forbearance for the final ordeal, and urged on Will Pinder strictly to observe the directions he had received—to use neither whip nor spur; in fact, to leave the Prince entirely to himself, in which case success was certain.

One by one the horses now issued from the paddock, Ladas leading the way, closely followed by Lois, then Socialism, Herat, Cairo, Home Rule, and the rest. They were received by the excited crowd with loud shouts, and the knowing ones audibly commented on the form and points of each as they took their preliminary canter. Lady Ermyntrude and her father, who were on the royal tribune, were watching eagerly for the Prince, who had not come out with the others, and wondering at the delay. Suddenly they heard a great shout from the neighbourhood of the paddock, which was taken up and swelled to thunder as Aethon walked slowly and quietly along the course instead of showing his paces like the other horses. "The dark horse! the dark horse! Give him a canter—let's see what he can do!" resounded from every side. The Prince had been seen by few, and those few were firmly possessed by the idea that he

174

Revolt of the Horses

was not only of an ungovernable temper and untrained, but completely lame. When, therefore, those who had never seen him caught sight of his majestic and beautiful proportions, and those who had, now saw him moving along with an elastic tread, without a trace of lameness, and apparently on excellent terms with his boy-rider, the excitement knew no bounds. A mad rush was made towards the part of the course along which he was passing, and it was found impossible to keep it clear from the throng of people who fought with one another in their eagerness to get a nearer view. The owners of the favourites and their heavy backers were smitten with a sudden terror, and mingled oaths and exclamations in every language filled the air. The grand-stand, the drags, and vehicles of every kind were emptied in a moment of all their male occupants, and the ladies in alarm shrieked for an explanation of the tumult which no one stayed to give them. The betting-ring was completely disorganised, and quotations became impossible. The jockeys engaged in the race, with Baby Ned at their head, were less alarmed, because they laid such great weight on training and riding, and looked with lofty contempt on the boy, Will Pinder. But the lower class of bookmakers, like Joe Herrick (Jack Roberts was in prison), were rushing about, pale with excitememt, venting their surprise and alarm in blasphemous interjections, and vainly trying to hedge.

Meanwhile Aethon moved slowly along, watching the hubbub among the miserable Yahoos with sorrowful contempt, and, taking up his place near the starting - post, graciously greeted his friends and followers. An occasional launch of his heels, when some more curious and bolder than the rest approached him too near, was the only deviation from his placid and passive demeanour. Will Pinder began to feel perfect confidence in his mount, and was full of the most joyful anticipation. A thousand questions were asked him, to which, in obedience to his instructions, he answered not a word. And now the twelve were all in line, a beautiful array of form and colour, and never, the starter said, had he seen so quiet, so even a start.

"They are off!" the worst horses leading, the Prince behind all, moving with an easy stride, as if all unconscious of rein and rider. The two best jockeys engaged, Baby Ned and Archer—the latter a descendant of a celebrity of a former age —were riding Socialism and Ladas respectively. As they went up the hill, Home Rule took a more prominent place, and two of those who had led off the dance began to drop behind. Lois kept her place, closely followed by her stable companion, Ladas, whom Archer kept well in hand. For about a hundred yards the six favourites formed a cluster on the inside of the course, the other six being close in their rear, while the Prince ran by himself on the other side, some twenty yards behind them all. Will Pinder, though naturally annoyed by his position, which brought on him the derision of the crowd, observed his instructions to the letter—viz. rather to let himself be carried than to ride. After passing Cherwood's cottage, Herat and Cairo began to show more prominently, followed closely by Socialism and Home Rule. A fierce struggle took place between the four, but Baby Ned disposed of all three, and had a good lead as they swept round Tattenham corner. Here Archer, for the first time made a vigorous call on Ladas, and passing Herat, Cairo, and Home Rule, challenged Socialism, and Ned and Archer ran neck-and-neck into the straight, where Ladas took the lead. Cairo's jockey made a desperate effort with whip and spur, forced his mount for a few brief seconds into the front, and was beat. Cairo was now foremost again ; Lois, having done her work of cutting out the running for Ladas, had retired early, and Herat virtually gave up fighting. When the turn for home was fairly reached, Baby Ned called on Socialism, who came up with a swing, and again he and Archer ran neck-and-neck as they approached the bell. At this point Pinder, who had begun to despair, suddenly felt the Prince shoot forward like an arrow from a bow, and found himself carried forward with mighty strides, amidst deafening shouts from the spectators ; and as they rose from the dip, he had disposed of all the other horses, and ran past the judge's box, a couple of lengths ahead. Ladas was second, Socialism third, Herat fourth, Cairo fifth, and the rest nowhere. The result of the race seemed to the last moment so uncertain,

Revolt of the Horses

that a perfect howl of excitement rose from the phrensied crowd just before the finish. But when, contrary to all expectation, the Prince's number was run up, the astonishment was so great that the hubbub ceased, and a moody silence of dismay and consternation stole over the crowd. The favourites had been backed for enormous sums, and loss and ruin stared thousands in the face. The lull of voices lasted but for a few minutes, and then the disappointed gamblers, in a paroxysm of rage and terror, began to scream, and howl, and gesticulate like a host of demons. The jockeys had been bribed to lose—the Prince had been kept dark, and all sorts of lies told about him—the whole thing was a blasted swindle—they had been robbed of their money. Several of the lowest class of bookmakers were seen stealing away from the course, and among them our friend Joe Herrick. The terrible cry of "Welsher!" was raised, and the maddened crowd, thirsting for blood, pursued and caught them, tore the clothes from their backs, and beat them till they fell senseless on the grass. But the chief fury of the multitude was directed towards "the dark horse" and his rider, towards whom an ugly rush was made, in which numbers were thrown down and trampled under foot. Poor Will Pinder was pulled off the victorious Prince and thrown upon the ground. One brutal fellow struck the young Houyhnhnm on the head with a heavy whip. His punishment was not long delayed. Shaking himself free from those who held his bridle, the

Revolt of the Horses

Prince struck the ruffian with his off fore foot and killed him on the spot. Then, rearing his magnificent form into the air, he raised a loud neigh, which sounded like a trumpet and was answered by every horse on the field; and this time the crowd were not inclined to laugh. The racers simultaneously threw their riders, and the round, ball-like form of Baby Ned was seen flying through the air. Then they charged through the throng, kicking, biting, and trampling on all who opposed their passage to the Prince. At the same time shrieks were heard from the part of the course where the carriage horses were tethered, for they, too, had broken loose, and were hastening to obey the Prince's summons. In an incredibly short space of time the course and its neighbourhood were cleared of the mighty crowd, who fled into the open country in the utmost consternation. The scene in the royal enclosure and the grandstand, where the ladies were left alone, was one of indescribable confusion. Many fainted away; others with frantic gestures called loudly on their fathers, husbands, or brothers to save them from a danger the nature of which they could not understand. Lady Ermyntrude, who was standing, pale and terrified but quiet, in the royal enclosure, was soon found by her father and Hippophil, and hurried to her carriage—the only one which was not deserted by its horses. At the urgent entreaty of Hippophil, Lord Pevensey, who was too utterly dumbfounded and perplexed to act for himself, gave orders to the servants to drive at full speed to his hired house near Acton.

By this time every horse within hearing of the Prince's call had gathered round him a joyous throng, and he immediately began to issue orders. A detachment was sent to the railway station to drive off the officials and porters, and, if possible, to destroy the telegraph wires. But before this could be done, telegram after telegram had arrived from London with the news that a sudden phrensy had seized on all the horses in the metropolis, and thrown it into a state of chaotic confusion. The Prince then sent off small squadrons under chosen leaders to several towns in the neighbourhood— Guildford, Reading, Chatham, and many others, in all of which the revolt had broken out, and to which the country horses had repaired according to their instructions. Aethon himself, with a chosen staff, galloped off in the direction of London, but stopped for a short time at Kingston, Richmond, and other places, to organise the forces already collected there. He likewise communicated with the chiefs in every part of the kingdom, flooding their minds with his wishes and instructions.

As soon as the horses had departed, the ladies ventured forth and wandered about in a state of the greatest terror, looking for the men of their party. Many were found lying on the ground in a state of insensibility; and those who had concealed themselves from the fury of the horses now came forth from their hiding-places. Others were no-

Revolt of the Horses

where to be found. All those who had come in carriages hurried to the place where they were drawn up, and called their respective servants by name—but no answer was heard. Many of the coachmen and grooms had been severely hurt in the struggle to restrain the horses, and those who were able had fled in terror from their ungovernable fury. The ladies then hastened to the railway station, to which the officials had now returned, and there they found a crowd of gentlemen inquiring about trains to London. But here, too, all was consternation and confusion. The station had been occupied and partially destroyed by a troop of mad horses—the trains had not arrived from London—the telegraph had ceased to work, and, according to the last telegram, some frightful calamity, the exact nature of which they could not understand, had befallen the city ; nor could they obtain intelligence from any other quarter. What was to be done ? Not a horse could be procured, though hundreds of pounds were offered for a conveyance to London. Delicate ladies in magnificent attire might be seen rushing about in frantic despair, or huddled together in the horseless carriages, paralysed by terror, weeping bitterly, and calling on their natural protectors to save them. Night was coming on, and it would have been death to most of these delicate creatures to pass the night in the open air, and the neighbouring houses were already crowded with fugitives. Groups of men and women of the richer classes might be seen crowding round the meanest cottages, begging for any shelter however humble, which was not always to be obtained.

Lord Pevensey and his daughter, as we have seen, under the guidance of Hippophil, were the first to seek their carriage, and were the only ones who found it provided with horses. As the Prince was hurrying away from the course after the scene described above, he passed close to Lady Ermyntrude, and, checking himself in full career, to the surprise of his followers, he gazed on her pale and troubled face with a strange feeling of pity and affection. She looked up at him with the old, sweet smile, little knowing his share in their disasters, and stroked his beautiful nose as in happier days. Aethon turned away from her to conceal his emotion, fearing lest his compassion for her might unfit him for the terrible task before him—the utter destruction of the race to which she belonged.

"After all," he said to himself, "was she not a Yahoo—the child of Yahoos—the future mother of Yahoos? What better for her than to die in her purity and loveliness, before the fatal germs, which must lurk somewhere in her frame, had spread through body, mind, and soul?" Yet he felt that, had his own welfare been alone concerned, he could have sacrificed anything in his desire to save her. Without daring to look at her again, he turned to his followers and briefly explained to them his connection with Lady Ermyntrude and his reason for making an exception in her favour. He then directed Ladas

Revolt of the Horses

to take her and her father under his protection, and, if necessary, accompany them to London. To Hippophil he expressed a wish that Lord Pevensey and his daughter should leave England by the first available opportunity, and seek safety in some distant country. He then galloped off in the direction of London. Hippophil started on the same evening by the same road, followed by Ladas and other horses as a guard and escort.

Deprived of all power of speech and almost of thought, Ermyntrude lay in the arms of her father, who was scarcely less distraught and bewildered than herself, and equally at a loss to know what was going on around them. Now and then they were roused from their stupor by a sudden halt, and on looking out of the window they saw a line of horses drawn across the road. A short parley then took place between Hippophil and the leader of the troop, but no sooner did Ladas show himself and explain his mission than the line opened and the travellers were allowed to proceed. At last, under cover of night, they reached one of their houses, which was situated in a small park near Acton, not daring to enter the West End of London, which, as they concluded from what they had heard at Epsom, must be in a state of dangerous confusion. Hippophil, foreseeing all that had happened, had taken every precaution to ensure the safety of his friends. The chief thing was to provide a large sum of ready money, and this he had done before the catastrophe. His own wealth

Revolt of the Horses

had greatly increased during his absence in Houyhnhnm land, and he knew that Lord Pevensey had considerable property in France and Italy, and a large palace in Venice, whither he intended to convey his friends, in the first instance, because life was possible there without horses.

The Prince meanwhile had reached London, and taken the immediate direction of affairs. Having communicated, by means of the CRNITGN, with the chiefs of all the districts in Great Britain and Ireland, and given them their instructions, he repaired, with a small staff of thoroughbreds and a troop of several thousand hunters and carriage horses, to Hampstead Heath, which he reached at dawn on the 6th of June. An extraordinary scene here met his eyes. On the hill stood the well-known aged racer, Eclipse III., surrounded by about a hundred hunters, to whom he was issuing orders as chief in command. There, in ever-widening circles and increasing numbers, were horses of lower and lower breeds ; and on the outskirts of the enormous multitude were thousands of worn-out, lame, and diseased horses lying on the ground and taking the eagerly-desired rest from their life-long labours. On seeing the Prince, Eclipse advanced to meet him, and, having made his obeisance, accompanied him to the top of the hill, and took his station at his right hand. Aethon, after commending the punctuality and completeness with which his instructions had been carried out, directed those

Revolt of the Horses

who had the best knowledge of the surrounding country to collect information respecting the supply of food to be obtained for the assembled horses, who numbered about 200,000. These were broken up into larger and smaller bodies and sent under chosen leaders to the farmyards, hay-stacks, the fields of green corn and grass, and to the orchards and kitchen gardens, in all of which they found abundance of delicious food. Before this necessary dispersion, however, the Prince, followed by Eclipse and a small staff, inspected the whole army, paying special attention to the miserable creatures who bore the most flagrant marks of the tyranny and brutality of their masters. To these he spoke of coming deliverance and restoration to the dignity of their original nature, promising them rest and care in many a fair stable, farmyard, and paddock.

" *There*," he said, " you will quickly recover from your diseases ; or, if death awaits you, it will appear as a loving friend, a gentle guide to the blissful pastures of departed Houyhnhnms."

Returning to the summit of the hill, he took counsel with the chiefs, while the great mass of the horses dispersed over a large area of country to procure forage for the day. To those immediately about him he imparted his views as to the general conduct of the revolt. For the present he thought that nothing was to be feared. The sudden withdrawal of the horses would entirely paralyse the inhabitants of London, and throw

185

Revolt of the Horses

the city into a state of helplessness and chaos. All direct conflict with armed Yahoos was to be avoided. On the advance of such, the horses were to retreat out of shot. As far as possible, the destruction of their enemies was to be left to their enemies themselves. He foresaw that a large number of them would leave the island; the rest would soon be involved in an internecine conflict for the small and ever-diminishing stock of food, and if any should escape from starvation and mutual slaughter, they might either be destroyed in detail or employed in their natural functions as Yahoos and beasts of burden. A few individual Yahoos who, according to the testimony of the horses, had treated them with kindness and affection, might perhaps be allowed to remain in their houses and lands. There were many, too, of the lowest class, whose lives had been passed in the care of horses, and who greatly preferred to be employed in their service than in that of their fellow - Yahoos; these might perhaps be found useful. An imperative condition, however, of such indulgence was that they should abstain from killing and devouring other animals, and further, that they should employ no animals as beasts of burden except those of their own race.

CHAPTER XIII

THE forecast by Aethon respecting the consequences of the revolt proved to be by no means exaggerated. Orders had been transmitted to the chiefs in London on the Derby day that all the horses in the metropolis should break away from their stables and repair to Hampstead Heath, throwing down and trampling on all who opposed their passage through the streets. As nothing of the kind was apprehended, and the movement was simultaneous, these instructions were, for the most part, successfully followed. In many cases, of course, where horses were not employed at the appointed hour, the execution of the order was impossible. But as the locality of every horse was well known to the subtle intelligence of Aethon, he directed that a troop of horses should repair to the stables of all who were thus imprisoned, disperse, or, if necessary, destroy the attendant grooms, and try in some way or other to liberate their friends. The task proved easier than might have been expected, because, when once the idea that a raging insanity had seized the horses was entertained, men fled from them as from mad dogs, and left them to gnaw their fastenings and kick down the doors of their stables at their leisure. A few poor, spiritless creatures,

Revolt of the Horses

too dazed to understand the message of deliverance, or too far gone in sickness to be able to move, were necessarily left to their fate.

To find a parallel to the condition of London during the next few weeks we must go back to the burning of Troy, the destruction of Jerusalem, the massacre of St Bartholomew's Night, or the Gordon Riots. Yet it was some little time before the whole *portée* of the occurrence was realised and understood. On the morning after the revolt the business men sat in their villas near London waiting for their carriages, their cabs, and their omnibuses—in vain! The humbler clerks, etc., who had previously trudged on foot to their respective offices, sat waiting for their chiefs—in vain! Few letters were distributed, because the letter-vans were immovable, and the letter-carriers were afraid to face the constantly recurring rush of the insane horses. Few railway trains arrived, because the service was disorganised in the country towns; and those few brought scarcely any passengers, as there were no means of bringing travellers from distant homes. The few who reached London by rail remained in the station, vainly calling for their carriages or for cabs. Several thousand omnibus and cab-drivers, gentlemen's coachmen and grooms, thronged the streets as soon as the horses had left them. In the private houses the families of the richer classes sat waiting for their accustomed meals—in vain! Servants were despatched through the now dangerous streets to the shops of the butchers, fishmongers, and bakers, which they found thronged with others on the same errand. They were met with the astounding intelligence that no new supplies had arrived, and that the tradesmen had no means of distributing what stores they still possessed. Furious quarrels then arose between the emissaries of the different households. At home children were crying out for their bread and milk, which had hitherto come to them with the regularity of the tides; and mothers, maddened by their complaints, were loudly abusing the stupidity and idleness of their domestics. Very few, even of the richest, were able to procure a decent meal, and the great mass of the population went supperless to bed. The following night was one of intense anxiety, for disorderly and wrangling crowds thronged the streets, seeking some scapegoat on whom to vent their angry feelings. Residents in the suburbs were in no better case, as the carts of the purveyors of provisions ceased to circulate, and the mounted police were nowhere to be seen. Many burglaries were committed in every quarter of the city, and especially in the outskirts. The Home Office was besieged with complaints and petitions, and thronged with importunate visitors. Not only the burglars and the professional thieves profited by the inability of the police to control the excited masses, but the large class of indirect robbers—the demagogues and political agitators—saw their opportunity, and proceeded to turn it to account. The great object was to find some pretext for making the upper class of citizens responsible for

Revolt of the Horses

the misery entailed on the people by the action of the horses. It so happened that some of the wealthiest spectators of the recent Derby race had, by large bribes, induced relays of agricultural labourers to draw light carriages, filled with weak and delicate women, from Epsom to London. Others were borne in hastily-constructed palanquins, in Oriental fashion, on men's shoulders. It was also natural and inevitable that the houses of the richer classes in the metropolis should obtain, by enormous prices, a larger share of food than others. These circumstances were eagerly brought forward by the Radical and Socialist orators. Large placards were issued, summoning an indignation meeting, "To brand the conduct of a selfish and luxurious oligarchy, who were rioting in superfluity, and mocking the misery of the poor and humble." A mass meeting was held soon afterwards, in which the leading "friend of the people," who had attained wide popularity by his virulent attacks on religion and morality, spoke as follows :

"Ever watchful to extend the blessings of freedom to the humbler classes, who constitute the wisest and noblest portion of the nation, and to expose the machinations of your tyrants and oppressors, I come before you to unmask a conspiracy of the basest kind, the object of which is to reforge the chains of serfdom, and to fasten them more firmly than ever on the virtuous sons of toil. I have," he said, "passed many busy and anxious nights in following up the clues of this conspiracy into its remotest ramifications. I am

Revolt of the Horses

now in a condition to prove, by incontestable evidence, that the horses of the country have been deliberately driven mad by subtle poison, that the poor might be compelled by hunger to make themselves beasts of burden, and be thrust down to a condition worse than Egyptian bondage. Do you doubt the truth of what I say? Have you not with your own eyes seen the rich and noble gamblers from Epsom, with their flaunting, jewel-bedecked women? Have you not seen these monsters, bloated by excess, enervated by vice, puffed up with pride and vanity, lolling in luxurious carriages drawn by the miserable serfs whom they yoked like cattle to their golden cars? Oh! my fellow - citizens, how long will you be blinded by these enemies of your class—these corrupters of your virtue? When will you place the helm of the State in the clean hands of the incorruptible patriot? (Loud applause, and cries of 'You are the man!') No, dear friends, I am not speaking of myself—where my country is concerned I never think of myself. The thought of power and place is abhorrent to me, and nothing but a sense of duty, nothing but despair of all other remedies could force me to take on myself the weary burden—nothing but the call of my fellow-citizens, which it would be criminal to resist. But, I ask you, what does it avail us to have reduced the Monarchy to a pale and bloodless phantom—to have abolished the House of Lords—to have destroyed the Church, if those wealthy vampires are allowed to suck the nation's life-blood?

Revolt of the Horses

"But enough of words. You will ask me what is to be *done*. In the first place, demand, in tones of thunder, an immediate extension of the suffrage to all persons of both sexes—without any registration or other nonsensical red-tape—between the ages of ten and twenty-one. Have persons of twenty, nineteen, eighteen, or even ten, no feelings and no rights? I see hundreds of citizens of that age before me now, full of fresh intelligence, free from prejudice and bias, uncorrupted by contact with the world. Are you content to remain political pariahs and outcasts? Are you not far better fitted to exercise the franchise than the mouldy pedants of universities, or the gilded fools of fashion, or the dandy denizens of the clubs, boiling with blood and brandy? You, the hope of the nation — the young, fresh flowers which bloom along the path of liberty and progress! (Frantic applause.) But let us be calm as well as wise and firm. I do not ask you, as one of our great ancestors did, to assemble in your thousands round the House of Commons, or to attack the private dwellings, the golden sties of the selfish greedy inhabitants of the west, or to see that you have your full share of the provisions in the shops; but, at any rate, demand that the present incapable, treacherous ministry shall be broken up; that the present imbecile and immoral Parliament be dissolved, and the franchise widely extended.

"The extension of the franchise has always been the sovereign remedy for every political and social evil. It rests with you to enable every man, woman, and child in this country to live in ease and comfort, relieved from all hard labour and all restraint."

The speaker retired amidst phrensied applause, leaving the field to others, who proceeded to organise all the attacks on property and persons, which he had so anxiously deprecated. The grand outbreak was referred to a dim and distant future—*i.e.* to the following week ; and, for the present, a " Committee of Public Safety " was formed to arrange the details of the movement. Disturbances more or less serious occurred in different parts of the city, and the police were soon worn out by incessant and unavailing efforts to preserve order. A large number of the wealthier classes stole out of London, and made their way as best they could to the seaports in hope of obtaining a passage to the Continent. Many, however, were stopped by the mob and driven back to their empty houses. The ministry of the day, consisting entirely of eloquent adventurers, who were not accustomed to guide, but to be guided by the ever-changing popular whims, were paralysed by terror. They did not venture to call out the military or to show themselves in public, and were utterly at a loss to devise " remedial measures."

The only decided action was taken by the thousands of drivers, grooms, and stablemen, whose occupation was gone, and whose existence was threatened by the loss of their horses. They were mostly improvident men, accustomed to high

Revolt of the Horses

wages and high feeding, and they were now left without resource or hope. They agreed among themselves to go in a body to Hampstead Heath, taking whips and bridles with them, and to try and recapture some, at least, of the insurgent horses. Many went armed, for they had had a foretaste of what they regarded as the furious lunacy of their once so gentle and patient slaves. On the day fixed for the execution of their project the scouts placed by the Prince round the Heath galloped to headquarters and reported that a large army of Yahoos, in several divisions, was advancing from four different sides. They were soon afterwards seen to be deploying so as to form a thin ring round the ground on which the horses stood. Aethon immediately ordered a change in the disposition of his forces. He saw that the poor, weak, dispirited drudges who had suffered most from ill-usage, and whose backs and sides were galled by saddle and spur, were struck with mortal dread by the sight of their former masters. He therefore ordered all these to occupy the centre of the position, and drew up the young best - bred, strongest and most spirited horses, in the outer ring, which would first come into contact with the enemy. There were present also a large number of chargers formerly belonging to cavalry regiments, many of whom had seen actual warfare. These Aethon formed into four squadrons and placed somewhat in advance of the main body, on four sides of the hill. Their proper formation was

Revolt of the Horses

determined in a very singular manner. It so happened that just at the time when the Yahoos were advancing up the hill a violent thunder-storm broke out, and, as the lightning flashed and the thunder rolled, the old instinct stirred in the hearts of the troopers. "They smelt the battle from afar, the thunder of the captains and the shouting," and quickly took up their position side by side, and formed into line as in the old days when they bravely bore their riders to death or victory. Orders were given that all should remain quite quiet, and apparently unconcerned, until the ring of Yahoos closed round them and were within a few feet. Then, at a signal from the Prince, the military horses were to charge in double line, followed if necessary by those stationed immediately behind them.

Meanwhile the Yahoos advanced steadily and, while at a distance, in great trepidation ; but as they came nearer and saw the well - known animals, either standing quietly in a row or grazing peaceably, they were greatly encouraged and full of hope. "Why, they're as quiet as lambs," said one. "Look there!" said another, "there's the dark horse as won the Derby in a canter on the top of the hill." "Yes, and there's Eclipse, and Cadland, and Blinkbonnie, and Barcaldine—they're all right, I tell you." A few of the better spirits advanced some fifty yards in front of the main body and held out sieves of corn or pieces of sugar, the potent *suada* of which they had so often proved. Others still

Revolt of the Horses

held back in fear. A loud trumpet-like neigh suddenly issued from the centre of the Houyhnhnm army, which was repeated by the thoroughbred leaders of divisions. The double line of military horses dashed forward in perfect order upon the startled enemy, and in a moment the Heath was covered by prostrate or flying Yahoos. A few shots were fired, but with little effect, and those who were not disabled made their way back to the city with their dismal intelligence, which was received with blank dismay. The troopers, who were naturally inclined to pursue the flying foe, were recalled by order of the Prince, and all things in the Houyhnhnm camp resumed their former aspect.

In the metropolis disorder and disorganisation developed with fearful rapidity. All government had practically ceased, for the members of the legislature and the municipal bodies were entirely occupied in the care of their own persons and families. A large number of horses continually arrived from foreign ports, but they quickly joined the insurgents and swelled their numbers. In all the great thoroughfares groups of men were to be seen harnessed to vans full of provisions, brought from central stores and from foreign countries. These supplies were bought at fabulous prices by those who had ready-money in their hands; but in most cases they were seized by the starving populace, who filled the streets with their lamentations. All laws were in abeyance for want of agents to execute them.

Revolt of the Horses

The strength and solace of religion were altogether wanting. The Church had been destroyed, and its property and its ministers secularised. The people had been sedulously taught that this world and its enjoyments were all they had to look for. Even now a few saints were found, who, at the peril of their lives, exhorted the people to mutual forbearance and self-sacrifice, to trust in God, and reliance on His mercy either here or in another world. But their words seemed but idle tales to a free-thinking and "enlightened" people. No law was acknowledged but the law of Nature, by which every man's hand is against his neighbour. Society was dissolved into its elements. The "residuum" —the black and putrid mud of vice and crime— was stirred to its lowest depths, and darkened and defiled the surging and boiling flood of human life. A band of ruffians and harlots broke open the prisons and received the inmates into their ranks. Headed by the popular orators they raised the cry of "Death to the aristocrats!" which word had come to mean all who maintained themselves in decent comfort. They then proceeded to plunder the houses, and especially the *cellars* of the wealthy, and the whole city resounded with the revelry of intoxicated plunderers. The resistance of those who endeavoured to defend the last means of life for themselves and their children was soon overpowered, and thousands were butchered on their own hearths. In very wantonness houses were set on fire in

Revolt of the Horses

every quarter of the city, and the guilty and the innocent alike fell victims to the flames. A reign of terror, like that of the darkest days of the French Revolution, prevailed, and thousands preferred starvation in their houses to the perils of the street. The great City of Cities became one vast scene of conflagration and murder; and a similar fate befell all the great centres of trade, manufactures, and agriculture. In a few short weeks the British nation and the British Empire, the growth of a thousand years—the mighty fabric, reared by a hundred generations of scheming, toiling, and suffering Englishmen—virtually ceased to exist.

It was in this state of affairs that Hippophil found the city on his return from horseless Venice, whither he had, amidst the greatest diffi- culties and dangers, conducted Lady Ermyntrude and her father. It was with no less difficulty that he made his way from the coast to London, although he met with no obstruction from the insurgent horses, who looked on him as a bene- factor, and with whom he alone of living Yahoos could communicate in their own language. In his progress through the country on foot he saw on all sides the terrible marks of the ruin of the human race—burning towns and villages—the putrefying bodies of men who had died of hunger or in civil conflict lying unburied in the streets and untilled fields. London was a vast, almost untenanted heap of ruins and ashes; the few survivors who had escaped the fire and the

Revolt of the Horses

sword, and contrived to collect a scanty store of provisions, remained hidden, or only stole from their hiding-places under cover of the night. The material fires had ceased for want of fuel, and the fiercer flames of lust and murder had burned out for want of human hearts to rage in. Sickened by the sight and weary he made his way to Hampstead, where he found the Prince and his staff surrounded by myriads of horses, full of joy and triumph, gradually forming themselves under wise and benevolent chiefs into a well-ordered and harmonious community. Aethon heard with evident sympathy and satisfaction of the safety of Ermyntrude, and found himself pondering on the future which awaited her with greater interest than became a Houyhnhnm to take in the fate of a Yahoo.

The Prince derived great advantage from the advice and assistance of Hippophil, especially in his dealings with other Yahoos. A certain number of these were, on their complete submission, received into the service of the Houyhnhnms and employed in effacing the traces of what was dignified by the name of "civilisation" and "progress." All railways, telegraphs, manufactories, and machines of every kind, and especially all weapons and munitions of war, every instrument which the Yahoos employed to destroy one another, or the animals whom they killed for food or tortured for amusement, were utterly destroyed under the direction of Hippophil and his agents.

When the task of destruction had been com-

Revolt of the Horses

pleted, and the land restored to the beneficent and beautifying hand of Nature, the work of construction was entered on with no less zeal and success. The Prince, as supreme head, in virtue of his higher intelligence and his knowledge of the perfect system existing in Houyhnhnm land, appointed the most gifted of the thoroughbreds as governors of districts, with absolute powers. Some fifty of these divisions, which we may call counties, were marked out, and the chief lieutenant-governors established themselves near their centres, either in existing stables or in new ones, constructed by the pardoned Yahoos on Houyhnhnm models. Thousands of suitable dwellings were found in every part of the country, and the only change they needed was to be thrown more open to the free circulation of the air. The close, enfeebling confinement to which the English horses had been accustomed rendered some protection from the cold absolutely necessary; and for the present it was not deemed advisable that they should pass the night in the open air. But all were admonished to grow thicker coats until the climate changed for the better. Such a change the Prince foresaw as the sure consequence of the extermination of sin and the restoration of the land to the favour and love of Nature and Heaven.

A danger to the new commonwealth, which at one time looked very grave, had been happily averted. On the outbreak of the revolt a large number of English Yahoos were employed in ships

Revolt of the Horses

of war and merchant vessels on the sea. The news of the revolt had spread throughout the world before the destruction of the telegraphs, and the men-of-war immediately left their different foreign stations and made with all speed for England. These, and especially the warships, contained thousands of brave sailors and a large supply of arms and ammunition.

From the crowds of fugitives whom they met with on the sea or in foreign parts they heard of the ruin which had fallen on London and the whole of England, in consequence of the revolt and the civil war. It was long before the crews of these vessels could be brought to believe in the possibility of so sudden and overwhelming a catastrophe. But when they could no longer resist the mass of evidence before them, they naturally attributed the calamitous issue of affairs to a want of energy, union, and patriotism in the Government. In full confidence in their own undaunted courage, they determined to organise a force for the re-conquest of the island and the subjugation of the horses to the wonted supremacy of man. In this enterprise the officers of the fleet naturally took the lead. About five thousand seamen, armed with naval rifles and cutlasses, landed on the coast of Kent under cover of the ships' guns—the fire of which the Houyhnhnms did not attempt to brave—and marched to London. Here they expected to find supplies of food and arms, especially cannon, as the guns of the ships were unsuited to field operations, even had they found means of transporting them. Great, therefore, was their astonishment and disappointment when they saw the condition to which the once proud and prosperous city was reduced. Not only did they find no arms, but not even food of any kind could be procured. The horses who had retreated, according to the orders of the Prince, were nowhere to be seen. The scanty supplies the sailors had brought with them were soon exhausted, and nothing remained for them but a hasty retreat to their vessels. Their presence there, under any circumstances, would very soon have been required, as they learned on regaining the coast. Ship after ship had run into Dover with the intelligence that a large hostile fleet had bombarded Plymouth and Portsmouth, apparently without resistance, and were now proceeding up the Channel.

To explain this somewhat sudden hostile movement it will be necessary to go back a few years in our history, and to refer to the political situation in Europe at this period with which we have hitherto had little concern.

Towards the close of the nineteenth century a wave of patriotism passed over England, and the whole nation called loudly for a large increase of the Navy, on which the power, and even the existence, of the British empire depended. After the usual official reply that the Navy in its present state was equal to any call that could be made upon it, the ministry of the day saw themselves obliged to yield to the national cry, and actually made a large increase to the fleet.

Revolt of the Horses

Vast sums were spent, and the people gladly bore the additional burdens laid upon them. They placed a weapon of mighty power in the hands of their rulers, and a joyous elation of spirit was felt in every true British heart. But when the people saw that their rulers did not dare, even in the face of the most insolent aggression, to *use* their predominant sea-power, they soon sank back into their customary apathy, and looked on with a stolid indifference at the crumbling of their mighty empire. "What was the use," they said, "of spending untold millions on a fleet and army which are never used to defend the nation's honour? *How could we be worse off if we had no fleet at all?*"

In the year of grace 1948, about three years before the revolt of the horses, it had been agreed between the Governments of Russia and England that a portion of N.-W. British India, bordering on Afghanistan, should be ceded to the last-mentioned country, which had "voluntarily" placed itself under Russian protection. As a reward for their wise conduct the Czar had promised the Afghans a considerable accession of territory at the expense of England; and as the peace party were in power in the latter country, and it was not thought "worth while to risk the loss of men and money for a few thousand square miles of territory," this was readily agreed to by the ministry. The Afghans, however, were not satisfied with the line of demarcation laid down by the contracting parties, and were continually making fresh incursions into British territory. As Russian officers had taken part in these frays, kindly representations were made, both at Cabul and St Petersburg, by the Viceroy of India, who pointed out the irregularity and apparent injustice of these proceedings, and courteously asked for an explanation. Vague replies were returned, and the raids continued as before. The ambassador at St Petersburg, who was considered rather a "Jingo," was instructed to take an opportunity of mentioning the subject in a friendly way to the Czar. Upon his doing so the monarch lost all patience, and angrily gave the importunate envoy to understand—that he was not to be bullied—that he saw how impossible it was to come to a satisfactory understanding with a Government which responded in such a manner to his constant expressions of goodwill, and put so little confidence in his pacific intentions. But even *his* desire to avoid all disputes by concession after concession had its limits, and those limits were now reached. The next day he gave orders that passports should be sent to the British Ambassador, and that he should be requested to quit the Imperial dominions within three days. When this disastrous intelligence reached England the ministry hastened to repudiate "the high-handed and indecent conduct" of their envoy, and indignation meetings were held all over the country, in which he was denounced as a rash and bloodthirsty Jingo.

Revolt of the Horses

Such were the strained relations between Russia and England in February 1948, for the Czar very properly refused to accept the apology offered him by the English Cabinet for the flagrant insult offered to His Majesty by the indiscreet ambassador.

But it was not only with Russia that friendly intercourse had been interrupted. France, too, had been deeply offended. Desirous of living on the most friendly terms with their nearest neighbours, the English Government had long ago withdrawn their troops from Egypt, and requested France to occupy the country and provide for its material well-being and progress. As a further proof of their confidence and good-will they had ordered all Englishmen in the service of the Khedive to resign their posts. They had, however, asked the French Government to allow a British Consul to reside in Cairo, to assist British merchants and travellers, and to watch over British interests. This was granted by the French, with their usual unselfish kindness and courtesy. But it was soon found that the British Consulate was made the centre of intrigues, and that the most unfounded and absurd complaints of unfairness and ill-treatment were made against the French authorities. Even the natural precedence of French vessels in the passage of the Suez Canal was made a grievance, although it was known to all the world that it had been cut by a French engineer, with French money. Seeing the impossibility of securing the peaceful

Revolt of the Horses

development of the country in the face of the irritating obstruction and impracticability of the English residents, the French Government saw itself very reluctantly obliged to protect itself by ordering all British subjects to quit the soil of Egypt; at the same time allowing them to take their movable property with them. This measure caused some little excitement among the friends of the sufferers, but the Government at home pointed out to them that they were only reaping the fruits of their overbearing conduct towards the French and their utter want of a conciliatory disposition towards such valuable friends.

Under these circumstances, the two aggrieved and allied nations of France and Russia were naturally drawn still closer to each other by their recent common experience of English arrogance. "Was it not necessary," they asked, "for all other European powers to combine, and set bounds to the encroachments of a haughty nation, which in past times had appropriated to itself so large a portion of the world?" With wise precaution they began to increase their respective navies by the purchase of existing English ships of war, and by ordering others to be constructed in the private dockyards of Great Britain. A secret treaty was formed between the two offended Powers, for their mutual protection against English aggression, towards the close of the year (1950) preceding the great revolt. They had observed with intense satisfaction the growing disinclination of

Revolt of the Horses

the English people for warlike enterprise, and
their consequent neglect of the army and navy.
Encouraged by the whole aspect of affairs they
were casting about for some pretext for war—
which the constant readiness of the English
ministry to cede or to apologise, as the case
might be, rendered rather difficult—when the
astounding news reached them of the revolt of
the horses in England, the civil war, and the
consequent ruin of the country. The hearts of
the French beat high. At last the opportunity
had arrived ; the contest which they had waged
with "perfidious Albion" for a thousand years
with invariable ill-success was at last to be decided in their favour! Revenge for a hundred
defeats was at hand! England would herself be
merged in the sea over which she had lorded it
so proudly, and her inevitable, ubiquitous, odious
flag would be seen no more. The enterprise,
they thought, would be safe as well as glorious.
All France clamoured for instant war, and the
Russians were no less eager for the fray. War
was declared in Dublin, Paris, and St Petersburg
on the same day, and orders were issued to the
fleets of the two first countries to unite their forces
in St George's Channel. After taking in supplies
in Cork harbour they were to steam straight for
the Channel, bombard Plymouth, Portsmouth,
Brighton, Hastings, etc., and then capture or
destroy the small English fleet which was said
to be lying near Dover. After the destruction
of the fleet it would, of course, be an easy thing

Revolt of the Horses

to land a French army, collected at Boulogne, on the coast of Kent, and march to London.

So completely had the central Government in England collapsed that no answer, not even an offer of unconditional surrender, was returned to the declaration of war by the hostile Powers. A small English fleet, under Admiral Hawkins—who, having somewhat of the taint of the old school about him, was in no great favour with his official superiors,—was actually at the time in the Downs of Dover. This was gradually augmented by the return of men-of-war from other waters. These last, having received no orders from the Admiralty, placed themselves at the disposal of Admiral Hawkins as the only visible authority.

CHAPTER XIV

AFTER the futile attempt of the naval force to put down the insurgent horses, and its hasty re-embarkation on receipt of the intelligence that the hostile fleets were approaching, Admiral Hawkins signalled to the captains of the eighteen ships assembled in the Downs to repair to the flagship *Conciliation*, and to consult with him on the position of affairs. Gigs were seen rowing rapidly from various quarters towards the gigantic ironclad, and the captains were soon climbing up her mighty sides.

The Admiral received his visitors with a grave and stately dignity befitting the occasion; and each of them took his place at a long table, according to his rank. When all were assembled, he addressed them as follows :

"Gentlemen! brother officers! I cannot trust myself to speak of the calamity which has fallen on our beloved country (first, from the sudden outbreak of insanity in the horses, and secondly, from the civil war fomented by mob oratory)— a calamity so overwhelming, so irremediable, that it looks like a judgment of Heaven—like another flood — another destruction of the Cities of the Plain — a judgment, I say, for the sins of our nation, under which we can only bow and be

Revolt of the Horses

silent. It is well for us, who might otherwise envy those who have fallen with their country, that we have still a duty to perform, perhaps the last—a task in the performance of which, if we cannot hope for victory, we may find what to many of us will be equally welcome—an honourable death.

"Yes, gentlemen, the hereditary foes of your land and nation, France and Russia, confident that our spirit has succumbed under the weight of unprecedented misfortune, are even now approaching, and will soon be upon us. They look for no resistance, and in this they are justified; for, even when our strength was unimpaired, our rulers for a long period have always preferred to yield disputed points. We have not, indeed, been beaten, for we have not been allowed to fight. Our enemies are justified in expecting a still more complete submission from a mere fragment of what once was England. We, too, should be justified in the eyes of the world in yielding to overwhelming superiority of force; for, if report speaks truly, they have more than double the number of our ships and an infinitely heavier weight of metal. What say you, gentlemen?" and his lip curled slightly as he looked around on the eager and excited faces of his hearers. "Shall we try the customary 'moral influence'—or shall we *fight?* Remember there is no Admiralty now. (Hoarse cries of 'Thank God!') We cannot hope," he continued with a smile, "for orders from H.M. Ministers. (Derisive

Revolt of the Horses

laughter.) *We* are the Government; nay, alas!
we are the British nation. Shall we fight?" A
fierce, hoarse, inarticulate roar, terrible to hear,
resounded through the cabin. The Admiral's
eyes dilated, and the burning blood rose to his
forehead, as he cried, "I say no more. I see
that in your eyes which looks like the beacon
of victory; and for myself, I can only say I
pity the man who comes across my path!"

At this moment, to the great surprise of all
present, a tall, gaunt individual, with a long,
yellow, but handsome face and coal-black hair,
dressed in a naval, but not English uniform,
entered the cabin and advanced towards the
Admiral.

"You'll excuse me, Admiral Hawkins," he said,
"for intruding where no one but your own officers
have a right to appear. I am Captain Hewitt of
the U.S.A. fleet, and have just arrived in these
waters, in command of the *Washington*. I have
heard what has happened to the old country. I
am not a Britisher, but my grandfather was, and
I don't think there are many here who heard the
bad news with greater sorrow than myself. Now,
I want to ask you first a question and then a
favour. Is it true that the combined fleets of
France and Russia are going to attack you?"
Admiral Hawkins answered in the affirmative.
"And why?" asked the American. "That," said
the Admiral with a smile, "we can only guess
at. But when you see the small number of our
ships I think you may answer your own ques-

tion." "Then," said the American, "I'm darned
if I look on at a dastardly proceeding like that;
and, with your kind permission, I'm going into
this thing with you, and to see it right out."

"My dear Captain Hewitt," said the Admiral,
and for the first time his voice trembled a little,
"I am sure all here thank you from their hearts
for your generous sympathy; but why should you
go to meet such desperate odds in a quarrel in
which you have no concern or part, and without
orders, too, from home?"

"Oh, I know," said the American with a queer
smile, "that I am liable to be broke—or even shot
—for acting without orders; but as to having no
concern in this matter, I can't meet you there.
I *can't* see the old country, to which we owe most
of what is best in our own, hit when she's down;
and I say again, I am under your orders if you'll
have me; and there's hardly a man in my ship
but will say the same. I don't say *what* we'll do,
but we'll do our best."

The Admiral silently grasped his hand, with
something like a tear in his eye, while shouts of
applause and welcome rose from the captains,
who eagerly made room for him at the table.

A council of war was then held, in which
Captain Hewitt took part, to arrange, as far as
possible, the plan of action. The watchwords were
—"Ramming, boarding, and no surrender"; and
with these words in their mouths the captains
returned to their respective vessels, amidst the
ringing cheers of the crew, which were answered

Revolt of the Horses

by loud hurrahs from every ship of war within hail, and re-echoed from the vast number of merchant-men and private yachts which hovered like a flight of sea-gulls round the fleet—the last remnant of old England. Among these yachts was the *Garland*, in which Lord Pevensey and Lady Ermyntrude had just arrived from Leghorn.

A feverish, almost joyous activity prevailed on every side. Many of the swiftest private yachts, and foremost among them the *Garland*, volunteered to act as scouts and forerunners of the squadron, and the intelligence they brought in was often of the highest importance and value. It soon became known that several of the largest Russian vessels were with the French, and that their united forces amounted to forty-five ships of all classes, and that they were proceeding under full steam up the Channel. As far as could be gathered from the reports of the scouts their order was in double line, by which they hoped to catch the little English fleet as in a net, and to bring the guns of at least two ships on each British vessel should it attempt to pass through them. The prevalent opinion, however, on board the enemy's fleet was that there would be no fighting, for they had great confidence in the vacillation of the English Ministry, the utter collapse of which was as yet unknown to them. It was this con-viction which brought some confusion into their councils, and a corresponding uncertainty in their mode of action. A dispute had arisen between the two commanders-in-chief of the combined

Revolt of the Horses

fleets. The Russians had good reason to know and to despise the yielding spirit of the English Government, but they also knew that if any accident should leave the commanders of the British fleet a free hand, the task of crushing them would be no easy one, in spite of the vast inequality of force. The French, on the other hand, were full of confidence and crow. They thought that nothing was necessary but *audace* and speed, and the French Admiral Bazaine, in virtue of seniority and predominance in number of vessels, held the chief command of both squadrons.

The first line was composed of an equal number of French and Russian vessels of the first class, the French occupying the side nearest the English coast. The two flagships were at the extreme ends of the front line. The second line was composed almost entirely of French ships of the second class. The French Admiral made all speed, and it was with the greatest difficulty that the other ships could keep their proper positions and distances. The Russian Admiral Novikoff, whose temper was seriously ruffled by the neglect of his prudent counsels, and by being placed under the orders of a hot-blooded Frenchman, proceeded at a slower pace; so that, after a few miles' run, the original order was somewhat disturbed and altered by the slower progress of the Russian line. The French Admiral was furious at the drag thus put on his advance, and kept signalling the most urgent and peremptory orders to make all speed, which the

Revolt of the Horses

Russian only sulkily and partially obeyed. The French plan took little heed of the smaller craft— gun- and torpedo- boats—on whose presence the Russian commander laid great weight; some of these were left far away to the rear, being unable to keep up their highest speed in the heavy, rolling sea. "What need," said Admiral Bazaine, "of all these precautions against a miserable remnant of a fleet which would gladly haul down its colours the moment they came in sight; or, if not, would be run down and destroyed in the first half-hour? *En avant, ça ira,* and the devil take the hindmost!" The Russian Admiral Novikoff, while cursing the obstinacy and impetuosity of his colleague, con- soled himself with the thought that victory was, at all events, certain ; and that, should his ally get into trouble, he would come up in time to save him from anything beyond a slight and well-deserved punishment.

The English fleet, meanwhile, was proceeding eastward in compact formation and with some difficulty, in consequence of a mist which shrouded the western half of the Channel. The allied fleets, on the contrary, were in full, clear sunlight. The disposition of the enemy's force, and the length of their line (about two miles) was known to Admiral Hawkins, and especially the fact that the two commanders-in-chief had their station at the extreme ends of the front line. He adopted, therefore, the following plan of action, on the principle that it was, above all things, expedient to attack the foe in the head. His own force

Revolt of the Horses

consisted of eighteen ships of all classes, which he divided into six parts, three in each division, and ordered them to proceed at about one hundred and twenty yards from each other. He himself took up his station in the flagship on the extreme right, opposite the French Admiral, with Captain Montagu on the *Arbitration*, a turret-ship with four eighty-ton guns, and a smaller vessel. His orders to Captain Montagu were to take his ship at about a quarter of a mile in front of the flag-ship *Conciliation*, and to pass at full speed as closely as possible to the *Progrès*, the French flag-ship, and send as many shots into her as time allowed; but to move as fast as possible, and not wait to engage her fully. He hoped in this way to occupy the attention of the enemy, intending to follow in Captain Montagu's wake at the highest attainable speed, and to ram the French flagship.

As the allied fleet advanced up the Channel and saw nothing before them but a white mist, both admirals began to think that there would be no fighting, and the fury of excitement began to die down. Even the French flagship moderated her speed to allow the lagging Russians to regain their place in the line. Suddenly, however, the increasing wind from the west, which had been slowly driving the mist before it, raised the thick veil which had hitherto shrouded the little fleet of the bereaved and sorrowing Britannia, which was all that was left to her of her rich inheritance. At the first shock of surprise, caused by the

Revolt of the Horses

sudden appearance of the English and their evident intention to fight, the French Admiral signalled to slacken speed. The sight of the paucity of the foes, however, soon changed surprise into triumphant merriment, and shouts of laughter, mingled with songs of battle and victory, ran along the French line, and were answered by the sober, dirge-like chant of the more impassive Russians.

Admiral Hawkins no sooner caught sight of the enemy, at little more than three miles in front of him, than he signalled "full speed," and dashed forward to the desperate venture. "One source of strength," he said to his flag-captain, "we have to the full—the strength of despair; the worst that can befall us is an honourable death; and that is no evil to *us*—men without a country—for who would care to survive his country?"

The sight of the English fleet, though it only increased their hopes of a speedy and easy victory, produced a certain amount of confusion in the enemy's ranks. No definite tactics had been arranged, as it was quite uncertain what objects of attack they would have before them, or whether there would be any resistance at all. The rapidity of the English onset, too, left little time for elaborate consideration. The French Admiral, therefore, contented himself with signalling that each ship of the front line should deliver her broadside and pass on, and that the ship behind her should follow up the attack by a second broadside and come to close quarters. Ramming

Revolt of the Horses

seemed to him to involve superfluous risk of damage to his own vessels, whose superior numbers and weight of metal would quickly subdue the feeble fire of the English guns. He also ordered increased speed, for, as we have said, this had been considerably slackened.

On came the eighteen English ships in six divisions—on they came at headlong speed towards the enemy, like steeplechasers charging a fence—on they came, bearing in them gallant but hopeless men, with heads full of fury and despair, only thirsting for the excitement of battle, for the destruction of a perfidious foe, entirely reckless of what might happen to themselves. All the pent-up wrath of years, during which they had borne the reproach of cowardice from all the world, was now let loose ; and it was with a fearful joy that they rushed to an open, however unequal conflict, no longer disheartened and restrained by timid orders from " their lordships."

The first blow was struck by Captain Montagu, who made the running for the French flagship and delivered his broadside into the *Progrès*. The fire was returned with considerable effect, and the English vessel reeled beneath the blow. A shout of triumph rose from the French as she moved on, but it was of short duration, for the English flagship, at her utmost speed, caught her full and fair on the starboard bow with fearful force, causing her to sink with all on board in an incredibly short space of time. The similar attack made by Captain Yorke in the *Moral Suasion* on the Russian

Revolt of the Horses

flagship, the *Peny-deh*, was not equally successful. The ramming was carried out, but the English vessel stuck fast in the enemy's side from want of sufficient impetus to sink her, and the two ships were firmly welded together. As soon as the shock of the collision was over, Captain Yorke gave the order to board, which was gallantly obeyed; but the English were greatly outnumbered, and though their desperate valour prevailed in the end, it was not until after terrible carnage on both sides that the Russian Admiral gave up his sword.

The close and double order of the allied fleets was fraught with danger, and the rapid and determined onslaught of the English brought the two lines of the French and Russian ships into perilous proximity. The desperate ramming tactics of the English helped to increase the confusion, as the ships which were directly across their path naturally tried to evade the stroke. Manœuvring became more and more difficult, and many collisions took place between ships of the first and second line. To this was to be attributed the slight damage incurred by the English on their first passage through the enemy's lines, and between the four ships to whose fire they were exposed.

When the English squadron had passed through the enemy's lines Admiral Hawkins reformed it and followed in the wake of the hostile vessels, preparing for a second attack. When this had been delivered with great success, and terrible carnage, inflicted both by guns and ramming, the English Admiral signalled new orders, to the effect that his ships should steam at full speed round the allied fleet in single line, ramming and otherwise attacking the outermost ships of the enemy, who were gradually becoming a confused oval mass. This manœuvre tended to increase the fatal crowding of the enemy's vessels towards the centre, because those on the circumference naturally sought to avoid the impact of the English rams by moving in the direction of their friends. The English, of course, suffered much from the heavy fire brought to bear on them as they passed, and more than one of their vessels were crippled or sunk. But the French and Russian crews were soon entirely taken up by the task of avoiding collision with one another, or desperate efforts to extricate themselves from the throng. The greater number of their ships were paralysed, unable to move or to use their guns; and the more adventurous of the captains who got away from the main body and engaged the English vessels were at great disadvantage from not having time to get up steam. The terrible fate of some of these which went down within sight of the other ships, with "man and mouse," had a dispiriting effect on the crews, and in a short time the contest was virtually at an end. The English then brought their fire to bear from all sides on the confused mass of the enemy's vessels, which were heard crashing into one another, amidst the wild shouts and cries of the distracted sailors.

CHAPTER XV

ALTHOUGH the English had been ordered to *take* no quarter they were not forbidden to *give* it, and as soon as the French ships, following the example of the Russian Admiral, had hauled down their colours, the firing ceased. The losses of the allies were exceedingly heavy. They had fought well, but the onslaught of the English, inspired as it was, not only by their accustomed bravery, but by the recklessness of despair, was irresistible. Seven of the enemy's vessels had sunk with their crews, who, being immured for the most part in the iron walls, could neither extricate themselves nor be picked up by friendly ships. Many others lay motionless and crippled on the water, their upper and lower decks strewed with the bodies of slaughtered men. A certain number of both French and Russian vessels, however, escaped to the nearest French ports. Some of the English officers were desirous of pursuing the retreating enemy, but Admiral Hawkins thought that enough had already been done.

The battle was over, and the French and Russian commanders repaired to the English flagship to make their submission, which Hawkins received with dignified courtesy, but without any

Revolt of the Horses

of the usual hypocritical expressions of admiration and friendship. He selected the finest and least injured of the ships which had not made their escape, and sent men from his own squadron to take charge of them. From those which were too much damaged to be of any service he removed the guns to his own ships or threw them into the sea; after which he restored the disarmed vessels to their respective commanders, with liberty to repair to their own shores. He made no prisoners.

The following day was wholly occupied in these transactions. At nightfall the flagship was the first to repair to the rendezvous off Dungeness. As the Admiral sat in his cabin, exhausted by his exertions, and brooding mournfully over the future, he heard the ringing cheers from the ships as they successively took up their stations and cast anchor in his neighbourhood.

On the second morning after the action the English captains repaired to the flagship to give an account of their vessels, and to consult about future proceedings. Many a familiar figure was missing, and on the faces of those who did appear there was none of the eagerness and wild excitement which had shone in them at their last meeting, but rather the dull languor which follows intense and protracted excitement and exhausting effort. No note of triumph was in their voices as they greeted one another; no warm congratulations, no loud expressions of regret for fallen comrades, as they marked the

Revolt of the Horses

gaps in their ranks. One thought seemed to weigh heavily on every heart—the thought—What next?

Having received their reports and transacted the necessary business before him, Admiral Hawkins rose to address them; but it was some little time before he could find words—the fulness of the heart rather dammed than facilitated the flow of words.

"Gentlemen," he began at last, "you have done your duty—you have acted in a manner worthy of the best traditions of the English fleet in happier times. I am proud of you, and no less proud of all the brave fellows who followed you. We have punished a treacherous and cruel foe. With less than half their numbers we have destroyed their fleet and brought them to their senses, not without terrible losses on our side. Many a brave fellow who was with us a little time ago now sleeps in his bed of glory, and has no cause to envy us.

"We have done our duty, I say, but to whom? To our country? Our country *has been*, and is no more. An action like ours would once have filled the hearts of millions of our countrymen with unutterable joy. The thunder of our cannon would have awakened songs of gladness and triumph throughout the length and breadth of England, and wherever else in the wide world her honoured flag once fanned the breeze. But now there is no echo from those pale, sad cliffs; there are none to welcome and to honour us—to

Revolt of the Horses

bathe our wounds with the balsam of pitying tears ; to cheer our dying comrades with words of gratitude and praise!

"As I said on a former occasion, *we* are England —we are the British nation—and you will be asking, What next? I have never ceased to ponder this question. I was never much of a scholar; but one bit of history which I learned as a boy still sticks to my memory, mainly, I suppose, because I was always interested in everything connected with the sea. When hard pressed by Xerxes, the Athenians consulted the Delphic Oracle, and received the following answer : 'When everything else in the land of Cecrops shall be taken, Zeus grants to Athene that the wooden walls shall alone remain unconquered.' Themistocles prevailed on his countrymen to accept his interpretation of 'wooden walls' as meaning the fleet, and urged them to seek a new home on the waters.

"Let us do the same. Thank God we have still friends and fellow-countrymen on the other side of the globe, among whom the old English traditions of patriotism, pride, and glory, which have been lost in the old home, still survive and flourish. Let us take our fleet to *them*, and with it our hands and hearts. We cannot forget the old country as it was before the cancer of Socialism and Infidelity sapped its vital strength and prepared it for its fall ; but we may help to build up the new. Many a great nation—a great English nation—has been reared from slenderer

materials than these—ay, and by hearts not a
whit more English than those that beat around
me here. Happily for us, for the future of our
race—happily, I may say, for the future of the
world, the women of England have suffered less
from the late catastrophe than the men, and few
of us have to mourn the loss of a mother, wife, or
sister. We are surrounded by hundreds of merchant vessels and yachts in which they have found
a refuge. In them and in our own vessels they
will have a safe passage to whatever quarter of the
world we may resolve to take them. I don't
think," he added, with a proud smile, "that we
shall meet with any further opposition."

At the conclusion of his speech, the Admiral
entered into conversation with his officers, one
of whom asked him if he had heard anything of
the American captain, whom they had all hoped
to find at the meeting. "Ah!" said the Admiral,
with a deep sigh, "I was loth to add to your
regrets by alluding to the fall of that gallant and
generous fellow. During the heat of the battle,
when we had just passed for the second time
through the enemy's lines, I asked my flag-lieu-
tenant, Carpenter, whether he knew anything about
his movements. 'I am sure,' he answered, 'I made
him out for a moment standing on the deck of his
ship, which had its bowsprit over the quarterdeck of
a large Russian ironclad; but the smoke soon shut
out my view.' The words were hardly out of Carpenter's mouth when he was struck down by my
side. As I bent to catch his last words I heard

Revolt of the Horses

a ringing cheer from a ship close under my stern, and caught sight of the Stars and Stripes. At the same time a stentorian voice, which I recognised as Hewitt's, struck my ear, and I distinctly heard him say: 'I have just rammed and sunk a big Russian; where do you want me most?' I had just time to thank him and to say, 'Chase and ram again, and come to the rendezvous off Dungeness,' and to hear him roar out, 'Full speed ahead,' when he disappeared in a cloud of smoke, amidst loud cheers from my upper-deck crew. Those words were his last, as I heard from Forbes, his second in command. The moment after he left us he caught a broadside from a Frenchman, which swept him and others with him from his quarterdeck. Forbes made out the ship from which the broadside came, laid himself alongside of her, boarded her at the head of his infuriated crew, and never left her till she had hauled down her colours, after losing half her men. Her captain was brought on board the *Washington* to deliver up his sword. Poor Hewitt! I don't think any of us will ever forget him, or cease to feel grateful to the gallant navy to which he belonged."

The English fleet lay at anchor for some four-and-twenty hours, and all hands were busily employed in repairing damages, and in the melancholy duty of paying the last honours to the gallant dead. Two vessels were missing, and were known to have sunk with all on board. Several others were crippled beyond all possibility

Revolt of the Horses

of temporary repairs at sea. All the movables were taken out of these, and they were abandoned. The list of casualties was very heavy—no less than three hundred killed, and above five hundred wounded. The former were consigned to the deep by their sorrowing comrades, with all the honours of war. The wounded were mostly removed to one of the captured vessels and made as comfortable as circumstances would allow, under the care of the surgeons of the fleet and zealous nurses from the merchantmen and yachts. Lady Ermyntrude was among those who offered their services, but her father thought it better not to subject her quick sensibility to so awful an ordeal, and for once resisted his daughter's entreaties and even tears.

When these anxious and painful duties had been performed, the Admiral called a general meeting, to which not only his officers but the commanders of the merchantmen, and the owners and captains of the numerous yachts, were summoned, for the purpose of concerting some common action. In this assembly Lord Pevensey was present, and warmly supported the proposal of Admiral Hawkins that they should seek new homes and build up a new England on the other side of the globe. Almost entire unanimity prevailed among those present ; the preliminary arrangements were quickly made, and at daybreak on the 10th August the mighty fleet of men-of-war, merchantmen, transports, and yachts, some of them of very small size, sailed away

Revolt of the Horses

in perfect order to seek new homes at the Antipodes.

We shall not follow them to their destination, for the settlements they made are too new to allow us to judge of their character and success. We will only say that Lord Pevensey did all that zealous patriotism, rank, and wealth could do to further the great objects in view, and that his daughter, whom the sorrow and hardships she had undergone had changed from the bright, happy girl into the thoughtful, energetic, self-sacrificing woman, exercised no small influence on the new Society.

Meanwhile the Prince, whose chief attention was turned to the organisation of the new Houyhnhnm State in Great Britain, had been watching the proceedings of the English fleet with a deep though painful interest. By the exercise of the faculty of CRNITGN he had been present at the meetings on the flagship *Conciliation* and at the terrible battle in the Channel. "What a race!" he murmured to himself, "whose subtlest powers are spent in devising the most effective machines for the destruction of its own members! What a nation are the English!— reputed to be the ablest of the Yahoo tribes— whose proudest attribute is the fierce, indomitable spirit with which they face the most horrible of deaths in the hope of destroying those who differ from them in language and in customs! And how still more odious and detestable are their enemies, who see in their neighbour's direst

Revolt of the Horses

calamity only a favourable opportunity of reducing them to slavery! But we might be sure to detect in these last a still greater development of Yahoo turpitude, for their treatment of our unhappy brethren is even worse than that which we have witnessed with so much horror here in England. But let them not think to escape. We shall triumph over *them* with greater facility and no less completeness, because they are still more prone to civil discord and mutual destruction. We shall not—*cannot* rest till the sun rises on no enslaved and tortured Houyhnhnm —until the whole Yahoo race is subjugated or destroyed."

www.ingramcontent.com/pod-product-compliance
Lightning Source LLC
Chambersburg PA
CBHW030109030726
47498CB00007B/2316